SCUPPERNONG

Best Wishes
- Weldon Payne
10/22/13

SCUPPERNONG

by

Weldon Payne

New Voices Series v. 27

FAP BOOKS
FLORIDA ACADEMIC PRESS, INC.
Gainesville, FL

Published in the United States of America by
Florida Academic Press, Inc. Gainesville, FL, September 2013

Text and cover by David Greenberg Communications, Inc.
Author's photo by permission of Chris Payne

Library of Congress Cataloging-in-Publication Data

Payne, Weldon.
   Scuppernong / by Weldon Payne.
     pages cm
   ISBN 978-1-890357-44-3
   I. Title.
   PS3616.A978S38 2013
   813'.6--dc23
                                            2013025814

Dedicated to the memory of Charles Scarritt and Hudson Strode, stalwart supporters of the written word, who encouraged hopeful writers to strive for excellence during those halcyon yet challenging days at The University of Alabama in Tuscaloosa. God bless them and those others who championed hope over despair.

Chapter 1

The boy stood barefoot in the shade of a Sumac bush at the edge of the field, waiting as Shack came down the row behind a plow, rolling the ground back in sleek, black slices. This was the first time the boy had seen it, and it was true, just as he had heard: Shack wore a coat and tie. A red rose was pinned to his lapel, and he was following the broad roan mare, breaking ground.

Shack had already pulled the rein and clucked to turn the horse before he saw the motionless boy. "Hey there, Jack Rabbit. You looking for me?"

The boy nodded.

"Well, I nearly-bout didn't see you."

"Ma sent me."

Shack pushed his hat—hard yellow, flat-topped straw with a dark red ribbon on it—back then took it off and fanned himself. His long, wavy hair was parted in the center. The hat had left a deep, wet ring around it.

"You from Blue Town?"

"How'd you know it?"

Shack fanned himself very slowly. "You ten years old, I reckon. Or nearly-bout."

"Day after tomorrow! How'd you know?"

"You Clink Stoddard's boy?"

The boy nodded.

"What's ailing Clink?"

"His bowels are locked."

"I figured." Shack fanned himself, still looking at the boy.

"Pa's about to die."

"Clink's bowels been locked since he was born, pert-nigh."

"Yessir. They worse, though."

"Clink's getting old."

"He's my pa."

Shack put his hat on and moved closer. "You love your pa, don't you, Chap?"

"Yessir."

"I believe you do." Shack's voice was low, gentle. He peered from under the flat hat. "The Lord'll spare your pa," he said.

"I hope somebody will."

"The Lord will."

"They give him up."

"You ain't."

"No sir."

"And your ma ain't."

"No sir, not yet. She sent me . . ."

"And I ain't."

"Will you come to our house?" the boy asked. "Can you . . ."

But he didn't get to finish the question because Shack had hit the plowed ground. His knees were sunk out of sight in the loose dirt, his eyes squeezed shut, and his hat was on its crown in the dirt. Shack was praying. There was a time for beseeching, and Shack believed in beseeching when the time came. His voice came loud and deep and spread across the field and scared the boy.

"Lord God of Abraham," he was saying, "raise up Clink! Deliver him, raise him up!" But he put too much emphasis on the last "up" and his horse lurched forward, headed for another round.

"Stop! Stop! You dumb, frog-legged critter, stop! Can't you see I'm praying?" There also was a time for chastising.

Shack jerked the horse to a stop and grabbed a dead cornstalk left standing from the year before in the yet unplowed parcel and whacked the animal across her muzzle. The mare reared, stepping across the traces, and the chain sawed high on her leg.

Shack stood quivering, holding the stalk tightly in one hand, bridle in the other, his teeth clenched, saying things to the animal that the boy could not understand, almost whispering. Holy things.

The boy had heard that Shack once beat a mule to death with a singletree, and now he believed it. He believed the other too, that Shack had shot a no-account farm hand long years ago and buried him in the loose coal-dirt of a railroad bed. He believed and was afraid. But the hand on his shoulder quieted him, and he was not afraid as Shack blew dirt off his hat and carefully adjusted it. Then, carefully, gently, Shack unhitched the straddled chain so the horse could step inside the traces again.

Watching, the boy saw something else—the stub of Shack's index finger on his right hand. So that was true, too.

Shack was still stooped when he looked again at the boy. The eyes changed color as the youngster watched. They went from black to blue, he was certain. Just as folks said.

"The Lord will spare your pa," Shack said evenly. "I will come to him tonight. Go on home."

And the boy went away, walking a few steps, then breaking into a fast run, going the long sandy run away from Shack and the mare, which now stood very still. He did not look back and so did not see Shack take the mare's head in his hands and kiss it.

Country ham was frying in the skillet, and Shack's wife was making red-eye gravy. Biscuits were almost done. She lifted a round stove-lid and thrust in a stick of wood, hammered it down, and replaced the cover. She pushed black hair off her forehead and wiped her hands on a blue apron.

Pearl walked like a child—quick, half-running steps carrying her from the sink to the stove, to the table, and then to an open window where she waited for the coolness. It was very hot with the wood-stove, but she liked to cook. Pearl always hurried, as though she thought someone was about to yell at her for not having done something. She was taking biscuits from the oven when Shack came in.

"You're hot," Shack said. "Just like you'd been plowing."

"Well, it don't make no difference."

Shack sat in a chair and took off his shoes. He held them so that loose dirt ran down to the heel. He walked behind the stove and emptied the dirt into a pan of ashes." I got a call to make tonight," he said.

"Who it is sick?"

"Clink Stoddard."

"I didn't know Mister Clink was ailing."

"Clink's bowels are locked," said Shack. "His chap talked like he's about done for."

Pearl wiped her hands on the apron. Shack took his seat again, next to the kitchen door. He leaned in the cane-bottomed chair so its back rested against the wall. He still wore coat and tie. He crossed his legs and looked at one bare foot. Dirt from the field lay thick on it. He wiggled his big toe.

"I'm going to him," Shack said quietly. "I promised the chap."

"I pity Miss Angie," Pearl said.

"The Lord'll spare him for Angie," Shack said. "Reckon could you arn my things?"

"They arned," Pearl said.

"Pearl, you work too hard . . ." Suddenly, Shack let the chair thump to the floor. He glared at the table. "How come you just got two plates set?"

Pearl stared at him as though she did not hear. As she looked, she saw the color of his eyes changing. "Wye, Murphy," she said, "It's just us. Just us two right now."

"Why?" he shouted.

"Well, it's . . . they ain't going to be here. Not yet."

"Where in hellfire they going to be?" Shack jumped up and leaped barefoot across the kitchen. "Where's Margaret, Pearl?"

"Wye, she's just gone town."

"How's she just gone town? I reckon she just up and sprouted wings and flown to town?"

Pearl tried to touch him, but he bounded away.

"Murphy," she said. "Murphy, she'll be back after while."

"Who'd she go with? There's no hiding it now!" His voice was louder than it had been in the field, praying. "You tell me who my little girl's out with." He shook a trembling finger.

Pearl stood beside the stove with a dish cloth in her hand. She took hold of the bread pan as though to move it. She answered him, but he did not hear, could not hear for his own voice. Finally, he hushed and glared at her, his eyes entirely blue.

"What have you done with her, Pearl?" he whispered.

"Oh, Murphy," she said. "Set down. You're tired out. Just set down over there and . . ."

"Ainser me!"

"Lottie. She's gone with Lottie."

"Lottie? *Lottie!* That little whore? My little girl gone town with that whore? Oh, my Lord have mercy."

"They just gone town, and I thought we needn't not wait. And Peeter's gone with the heifer . . ."

"I know where Peeter's at," Shack said. "Or where he'd best be. Better have taken that heifer to Sam's bull, like I told him. And he'd best be getting back here, too."

"He will, Murphy," she said. "He'll be here in no time. I didn't see no cause to wait. I knew you'd be tired out and . . . the bread's getting cold, Murphy."

Shack stomped out of the room. He went through the house, raging. "The whoremongers!" he yelled from the bedroom. "The low-down fornicating whoremongers!"

Pearl sat at the table. She traced a finger around the green border of a thick white plate. Eventually, Shack returned to the kitchen, barefoot and still wearing the coat with the faded rose in the lapel. He went outside and came back with a tin pan of water. He sat on the floor and washed his feet and slowly dried them with a flour-sack cloth.

"Some day," he said, without looking at her, "you won't have to get all hot over that stove."

"It ain't all that hot."

"We'll get one of them lectric stoves after we get the place," Shack said. "One of these days we'll get the place and then you won't have to get all hot and sweaty."

"I'll warm the bread," she said.

"The girl'll be back before dark, won't she?"

"Oh, sure."

"Lottie ain't no good girl," Shack said. "She ain't no girl for Margaret to be with."

"They just gone to get material," said Pearl.

"Yeah, but you never know who they'll see. You never know atall when she goes with Lottie. Lottie ain't no good."

"Well, Margaret is."

"I know she is, and I aim for her to stay good."

"She's a good girl, and she don't never go no place much," Pearl said. "All this time she's never gone no place hardly."

Shack took Pearl's hand. Just for an instant he held it in his rough paw, then he went to the door and threw the dirty water into the yard.

"Pearl," he said, after he had sat at the table. "They's just two things in this old wicked world I want. I want to serve the Lord God of Abraham. And the kids . . . I want them to be good."

"They all right, Murphy," she said. "I reckon they good as most kids. They grown up, is all."

"They's so much meanness in the world."

"But they good young'uns."

"I ought not sent that boy off for that," Shack said.

"I don't see why not."

"It's a man's job. Ain't no job for a boy." He looked a long time at the table. "No sir, ain't no job for a boy to be bulling a heifer. Can't tell what kinda thinking it'll lead to."

"Well, he's sixteen," Pearl said.

Clink Stoddard had been abed seven days and seven nights. He had tried laxatives. He had taken castor oil, calomel tablets, Epsom salts and hot water and tea and water boiled off oak leaves, and enemas, but nothing had coaxed his bowels to function. Clink did not believe in doctors; he was nearly dead.

Clink had been plagued all his life with bowel trouble, but always before he had been able to overcome it. Now he was dying, and his neighbors in Blue Town had come to face it with him. A carpenter, Clink had built the room where he now lay dying. The room was attached to an older house—the house where he was born—but he had never finished the ceiling.

Now he lay on his back and saw the dark rafters that for eighteen years he had planned to hide with plywood. It was one of many things he would never do. Where had it gone? Where had it all gone since the days when he had played in the other part of the house? Where were all the days and nights that had led to this twilight time when the flame from the lamp glowed softly and voices hummed and whispered in the shadows—the old tired, hushed drone of the Blue Town neighbors who had come to wait with him?

Angie sat to one side. Clink heard her shrill voice saying, "There ought to be something. He's suffering awful."

Other voices were saying, "The Lord's will" and still others: "Do you think he'll come?" And "What can he do?" And "I wouldn't have called *him* if it'd been me." And another: "He's got the power, though. Shack's really got the power."

"I don't know."

"I don't know."

In the yard the men stood talking. They, too, knew that Shack had been summoned.

"My old lady trusts him," one said. "She shore as Gawd trusts him. He taken a garter offen her throat bigger'n my fist."

"You mean goiter, Onnie."

"Whatever they want to call it, he taken it off. Just went and told her she's going to have to do what he said, and she said she trust him. You know what he done? Took and stretched a black sock around her neck tight as a belly-band—she turned right blue-like, and I thought he's choking her shore—but he taken and held it that away for a long time and said some stuff to her, and that there garter went away like it never been there. I wouldn't believe it, 'cept I seen it."

"He took a scorp'en out of the leg of one of my chaps."

"A scorp'en?"

"Big ole scorp'en. It was causing the chap to thow a heap of fits, but since then he ain't never had another fit or nothing."

"I don't know about people," another voice said. "But he driven rats away from my place. I ain't never had no truck with ways sich as his, but I'll say this, he driven ever last rat away from my barn. Run 'em clean off, he did."

"Better git him to my place then, reckon."

"Me, too. Nothing short of a far would get shut of rats in my barn."

"All I know's I ain't seen airy rat in over a year now. Used to be they's under my barn nearly-bout big as shoats. One day Shack stopped by my place, been grinding some corn. And I told about the rats. Well, he said he'd tell me how to get rid of every rat for good. Said if I's to take and write—now it sounds looney—but if I's to write them rats a letter on note-writing paper . . ."

"Hellfar, Daniel, what kinda letter?"

"Just hold your tater, and I'll tell it. Letter asking them to leave . . ." A burst of laughter interrupted him.

"Laugh all you want, but I done what he said. Said ask 'em to leave and put the letter out in the barn where they could get to it and sprinkle a little cow feed on it and them rats would come and eat that letter and they'd go away. Wellsir, I was just like you'uns, but I figured it wouldn't hurt none, so I done it. Next morning wasn't nothing left but a little ole scrap of my letter, and I seen one rat—seen his tail as he scooted into a hole—and I ain't seen another to this day, and that's been over a year."

And so on, as the night crept away, they talked, and the flame glowed inside, and the women talked, and Clink lay waiting to die, and the midnight hour was close at hand. Suddenly they heard hoofbeats thundering into the yard. They heard, but they scarcely moved. They didn't have time to move.

It was Shack, astride his big roan workhorse, riding in the moonlight. He wore a long white coat and white trousers, tucked into black lace boots. He wore a black string tie and a wide white hat. Before the horse had stopped, Shack touched the ground and with one leap hit the wooden steps and bounded onto the porch, a pistol in each hand. With two steps he was inside the old hall, firing both guns into the unfinished ceiling.

Into Clink's room he bounded, firing off shots into the rafters and shouting crude but direct orders pertaining to Clink Stoddard's bowels. The blend of pistol-shots and his booming voice vibrated in the room.

The women screamed and scattered away from the bed as Shack fired twice more, urging Clink to comply with his commands. The bullets ripped into the old feather mattress on each side of Clink. Shack crouched at the foot of the bed, eyes fixed on Clink.

Clink's eyes filled with tears. A broad smile cracked his face. "Bless you," he whispered, trembling. "Bless you, Brother Shack."

Slowly Shack blew the smoke away from the guns and put them in their holsters. He looked around the room, staring at each person and at all of them. No one moved. "Care for him!" Shack commanded. Then, in a different voice, in a very low, very soft voice: "Care for him."

Shack whirled then, and in three giant steps was on the porch, the steps, and then astride the horse again, riding fast into the night.

#

Chapter 2

Scuppernong, Alabama, lay in the shadow of Cat Mountain, a random piece of the Appalachians that had crumbled southward. The dead of one hundred and fifty years slept in the red clay at the base of the elevation. Near the graves, like a burnt cardboard box not yet fallen, crouched Primitive Baptist Church.

Farmers still worked the fields with mules; corn grew in the spring, and cotton blossomed white in the fall. A grader from Whitt City scraped the dirt roads now and then; dust swirled from passing cars in summer and settled on the houses and on rambling briars and blackberry bushes beside the roads. The people went their unhurried way. Kids rode a yellow bus to Blue Town after Sutton School was abandoned. Baptisms took place in Rainbow River, which wound around the base of Cat Mountain. It was a place largely unchanged, even by the war—a pocket of poverty and superstition and backwardness. Like every other place in the world, Scuppernong had its share of good and evil.

Red gasoline sloshed in the round glass tops of two gas pumps outside Bud Anthony's store, and boys loafed around the grease rack. Inside was a long white case filled with bologna and wieners and hard yellow chunks of cheese and pork sausage and pickled pigs feet. The wooden counter was soaked dark with grease. A metal ice box held Grapicos and Royal Crown Colas. Work gloves and extension cords were stuck on the walls, and the shelves were crowded with canned groceries. A long curled piece of fly-paper, loaded with black casualties from previous summers, hung from the ceiling back of the dark greasy counter.

Shack lived in one of the frame houses between the store and the mountain. Aunt Tessie Johnson lived in another at the end of a little gray road winding into the woods below the graveyard. Bottles, tied by bits of string, dangled like fruit from limbs of a scrub sapling in her front yard. Petunias grew from a black wash pot next to the steps. Two high-top work shoes, filled with dirt and painted blue, sat on the front porch as flower pots. Wandering Jew grew out of them and spread over the old planks.

Just before dark one evening, Aunt Tessie was sitting on the porch in a rocking chair, singing: "Never grow old. Where we'll never grow old; 'Tis a land where we'll never grow old."

Flank Busby heard the singing before he could see the house. There were no lights. He stopped in the yard. "Aunt Tessie?"

The rocking stopped. "All right?"

"How you, Aunt Tessie? This Flank." He stepped upon the porch. "How you getting long?"

"I tell you I ain't doing one bit of good. Old bones aching all the time." Her voice sounded very old and dry. "Ain't nobody'd care, I don't reckon, if I was to set right here and die."

"Shoot, Aunt Tessie, you know I would."

"You the only one then. If *you* would. Find you a seat."

"Ain't you scared, setting out here in the dark?"

"Pshaw."

"Somebody's liable to knock your head off."

"Listen. Henry won't let nobody bother me," she said. The work shoes had belonged to Henry—his last pair—and they had been on the porch before Flank went into the Navy the last year of the war.

The old woman rocked and hummed. She stopped and cleared her throat. "You scraped up a job yet?"

"No'm. Ain't found nothing."

"You looked?"

He snickered. "Yes'm."

"Beats me how a feller eats without working. Listen, Henry always worked. You ain't looked, I betcha. Done nothing but drank liquor, I 'spect."

"Aw, Aunt Tessie."

"I mean it, Boy. You better leave it alone. Listen to me."

"Little bit along chases the blues away. You ever have the blues, Aunt Tessie?"

"Blues? Pshaw! You better leave it alone. Listen, it'll ruin you. You young, Boy. I wouldn't touch it, if I was you. You hear?"

"I just sip a little to keep down the dust," Flank said.

"Hmmm. I'll tell you now I've seen what it can do. I had a brother—Bethel—went out of his head on account of liquor. Listen, Henry never touched it, I can assure you of that."

Flank yawned loudly. "Reckon when's it going to rain?"

The old woman ignored his question. "Sister Busby wouldn't want you drinking," she said. "She'd turn over in her grave if she knew you was. You hear me what I'm telling you?"

"I wouldn't do it if she was still here."

"Why, your old mama would rather seen you lay a corpse than seen you take a drink of liquor."

"I know it. Nobody cares now, though."

"Hmmm. I bet you drank plenty of it over yonder."

"Aw, chased the blues a little, Aunt Tessie."

"You didn't mess with none of them wild yellow gals?"

"Naw."

"What? You didn't, did you?"

"You know no gal wouldn't look at me, Aunt Tessie."

"Leave 'em be!" she exclaimed, coughing. "Will you hear me?"

She started humming the hymn again and then stopped abruptly. "Listen. Bethel went clean out of his head." She paused, and Flank heard her false teeth move. "You know what caused it? You know what driven him clean out of his head, Boy? Liquor, that's what. Listen. Damnable liquor. It'll kill you. It'll bite like a rattlesnake."

She started rocking again and singing: "Never grow old. Where we'll never grow old . . ."

After awhile, Flank stood and stretched. "Aunt Tessie," he said. "Reckon you could let me have a little bit on credit? I got me a job lined up tomorrow. Got to see a feller. I'll pay. Honest."

She rocked a few times. "Pshaw, Boy," she said. "If you bound and determined." She got up and went inside the house, walking slowly and with a limp. Shortly, a light flickered and then glowed dimly.

Flank waited on the porch. He thought of the tall and stooped old man who used to wear the high-top shoes. Henry was never very friendly toward him though Flank liked him. Henry was always walking in the yard, his head lowered, seemingly in thought. That's the way Flank remembered him. He wore broad green suspenders.

In a moment the old woman came back, carrying a coal-oil lamp in one hand. She looked very small in the light.

"Bound and determined," she said. "Hell-bound, sure's the world. Long-gone and short-coupled." She handed Flank a fruit-jar of rot-gut. "Listen. I'd take it and pour it out," she said.

"I aim to," he said. "I'll go right straight and pour it out."

"It'll kill you," she said. "It stingeth . . ."

"Thank you, Aunt Tessie. I'll pay you now just as soon as I get to working, honest to God I will."

Before he got far down the road, Flank heard her old dry voice singing again, singing about not growing old. He stopped and poured some of the whisky out, screwed the top back on, wiped his mouth, and walked on down the road.

#

Chapter 3

Born and reared within ten miles of where he now lived, Shack had never ventured far. For years a hard-drinking carouser, he converted after a near-death experience on a railroad trestle and was now looked upon as a preacher of sorts. He no longer worshiped at the Primitive Baptist Church or with the Methodists. He called himself a Thurs-Day Adventist now and attended church on Thursday in the old Sutton schoolhouse. When anybody else was there, Shack preached to them.

After his conversion, Shack hadn't been satisfied with what other preachers had to say. He read the Bible as best he could and had his own ideas about what it said. He thought Noah had struck dry land on Thursday, and this was his reason for being a Thurs-Day Adventist. He said if Noah hadn't struck dry land, mankind would have been in more or less of a fix, so Thursday was the logical day to worship.

Pearl went with him on the Thursday after he called on Clink Stoddard. Margaret and Peeter went, too, as did Clink and Angie and a few other people. They met at daybreak. Shack wore a coat, a wide tie, and a red rose.

That morning, Shack had them all do what he did when he attended alone: They sat quietly for more than an hour while outside, birds were singing. Shack sat on the floor in the rear.

Peeter wished they still went to the church where they had a piano that Mrs. Mayhall played with loud, thumping chords. It was strange coming here before school and waiting to see what his father would do. He wished Carol was there with him. Or somebody besides Mama and Margaret. The sight of Pearl's hard fingers gripping each other made him feel sad. He slipped a hand into his pocket and felt small pieces of smooth, thick glass he had found. He fingered these, choosing a dark purple piece that had been the round center of the bottom of a little jar. Peeter squeezed it between his thumb and forefinger. After awhile, he took it from his pocket, cupped it in his hand and peeped at it in his fist. He sighted through it at the sunlight beyond the window. It was very pretty and felt smooth and good to his fingers. It felt like the way he *felt* about Carol.

Peeter liked pretty things. Once, he had collected a huge paper sack full of feathers. But Shack, in a fit of anger, had thrown them in the fire.

Carol Argo. C.A. Black bangs. White teeth. Yellow pleated skirt, tight around her little round tummy. White sweater covering her titties like bunnies burrowed under snow. Maybe, later at school, they might happen up in the cloakroom, just the two of them. Might kiss her rose lips. Might say I love you. Might. If only there was ever a chance with nobody else close.

He wished he could take Carol to the picture show in Whitt City. He wondered what it was like inside the lighted theater; what it would be like to go there with her. He thought of a screen like the one in a corner of Henry Pitt's pasture where cars parked, and people watched picture shows. Shack said picture shows were sinful, but Peeter had seen, from a distance, the jumping figures, and one night he had seen them closer. That night he had slipped from bed and gone to the pasture and sat behind the cars, watching. He had returned late and could not sleep for thinking of the colored horses and rock cliffs and smoking guns and of himself crouched behind one of those rocks, ducking and firing his blue guns and of course Carol Argo crouched nearby. It had been a glorious, magical night, and the only reason he had not gone again was that Shack had found the loose window screen and repaired it.

Now, while birds sang, Peeter thought about sitting in a dark theater beside Carol, watching the magical multi-colored figures, and of touching dear sweet pleated-skirt Carol.

Pearl was praying when she heard the birds. "Lord, hep me be a good wife and not aggravate . . ." Then she heard the birds, and it reminded her of spring mornings in a little house before the

children came; mornings when she and Shack were awake in bed
with breeze blowing across a pasture and moving white curtains.
All those mornings with him. All those nights.

It had been so simple for her back then, had been before they
married. There had been no other man before Shack, but as a
young girl, giving in to the older, care-free Shack had been easy
and natural and quick. It had always been quick, but now . . . now
they didn't even share the same bed. What had she done? O Lord
what? Tears came to her eyes. O Murphy! Murphy!

In the path of the breeze, they had lain on the bed. But now.

O Murphy! Murphy! Her tears would not go away. Nor
could she pray.

Margaret sat apart from Pearl and Peeter. She wore a chartreuse
blouse she had made and a dark blue skirt. As always she was uncomfortable now that she was there and wished she were home.

Wish I hadn't wore this thing, she thought of the blouse. It was
the first time she had worn it anywhere. At home, in front of a
mirror, she had thought it was pretty; now she was sure that Angie
and others were making fun of her.

Little red circles on her milky skin showed where she had
plucked her eyebrows that morning. She thought of the lipstick
she had worn last night. Lottie gave it to her, but she would never
wear it outside her bedroom. She had bought a tube herself once
and used a little before going to the supper table. Shack had taken
a wash cloth and scrubbed it off, rubbing hard so that her teeth
cut into her lip, and shaming her the whole time for "putting that
devil's salve on."

Last night she had looked forward to coming to church. Long
after she had gone to bed she had thought about it; thinking that
maybe somebody would be there. Maybe some good-looking boy
who would sit beside her and walk her down the dusty road when
church was over. Nobody was there. Margaret looked at the open
hole to the loft in a corner of the ceiling. Two wasps flew around
the dark opening.

Even if there had been somebody, he would not have looked
at her, sitting there in that ugly blouse. And Mama drawn up like a
sick chicken, scared. And Papa back there on the floor. Old fool.

Margaret was relieved that Flank Busby wasn't there, like she'd hoped. She and Lottie had seen him in town, and he had wanted to talk with her, but she wouldn't talk to him. Lottie said he was drinking, said he stayed drunk half the time. Margaret didn't know whether he was drunk. But what would he think now if he saw her on that old bench and Pearl drawn up, cutting her eyes toward the window? And Peeter slouched by the window with his hands in his pockets? Mama's darling. And Papa setting back there on the floor. And in a little while he would be talking. Up there in front of everybody. Wish to the Lord I'd stayed home. Lottie makes fun, too, probably. Like they used to in school. In the auditorium. A long time ago. Giggling. Giggling as she walked behind Shack that last morning, head down, following him out of the school and home. Out of school forever in the eleventh grade. We was just talking.

Andy was the only one worth talking to. Practicing that silly play. Everybody else on stage, and Andy saying, "You know your part so good, Marg. Wish I knew mine like you." Nothing. Just saying things like that every day while waiting to give their brief lines. Saying: "I like that sweater, Marg." Holding my hand, maybe. Then Shack had come.

Mama was sick, and he come to get me to cook. Come and said, "So this here's what you're doing!" Said it so loud everybody heard. Then said all the rest so they could hear, too. Said: "I knowed it! I knowed it! Knowed it wasn't nothing no good." And then he said to Andy: "I know what you doing, Boy! You git on away from my little girl." I heard them all giggling. Maybe his arm was around me. Sorta. Or had been, I guess.

Now Margaret sat erect and rolled her eyes so she could see some of the others without turning her head. A faint smile played on her lips. She heard birds singing. She imagined them singing outside a hospital: And Margaret lies on a white bed, dying. Her face is beautiful against the pillow. She does not cry out in all the pain, does not even ask for water though her fever is great. Papa comes and stands beside her bed. He is crying. Forgive me, Baby! And Mama hugs her and says: "I love you, dearest Margaret."

And Peeter has to stay outside. "Forgive me, Baby!" But Margaret looks at the ceiling and doesn't say anything. She will be dead in a few minutes.

Margaret took a deep breath and looked at the dark hole in the ceiling where the wasps were flying. Suddenly Shack was walking down the aisle, slowly, and singing a hymn. Clink and Angie started singing, too. Margaret would not sing. She glared at the back of her father's head as he made his way down the aisle. When he reached the front, he stopped singing and stared at each of them. Then he started reciting slowly, distinctly and low: "Ye have heard that it was said by them of old time, Thou shalt not commit adultery; But I say unto you that whosoever looketh on a woman to lust after her hath committed adultery with her already in his heart."

His eyes swept the small band. He looked toward the ceiling as though trying to remember. Finally he started again, speaking very low, saying: "And if thy right eye offend thee, pluck it out! Pluck it out and cast it from thee. Thow it away! Because it is profit-able for thee that one of thy members should perish and not that thy whole body should be cast into Hell."

Peeter liked the sound of his father's voice although it made him nervous. He was always nervous when he was around his father.

"Now listen, People," Shack said. "Now listen to me. If thy right hand offend thee, cut it off! And thow it away!" He raised his right hand for them to see. "Do you hear? If thy right hand offend thee, cut it off!" He pulled his right sleeve away from the wrist, and spread his fingers. Then he bent all the fingers except one, leaving only the stub of his index finger, feebly pointing.

"See that?" He looked into each face. "You see that?" They all knew the story of the index finger, yet each person watched attentively. Peeter's face flushed darkly.

"I obeyed," Shack said. "Seven years ago this coming December I obeyed. I chopped her off. My own fanger."

He turned the hand, admiring the nub. "I cut it off," he said. He looked at them. "I would cut it off again. I would be obedient again." He stepped closer to them.

"Y'all know I used to be the best squirrel hunter around. Everybody that knows me knows it. Y'all know there wasn't nobody who could shoot a rifle better. You know that. Know I could shoot squirrels when nobody else could." He stopped talking and looked away, as though listening.

In the quietness, Peeter thought of an evening long ago when he had gone into the woods with his father; late in the day they had gone and sat quietly on a log and then Shack had whispered and pointed to a dark spot on a high limb and placed the rifle in Peeter's hands, and he had shot and missed—"Aim higher, Boy"— and shot again, and the dark spot had fallen, and later he and Shack skinned the squirrel beside the barn. Warmly, Peeter remembered.

"I loved it," Shack was saying. "I pure dee loved to shoot squirrels. To kill them. *Kill.* That was the thing. We had pork to eat. It wasn't the eating. It was just killing 'em. I said I'd quit. I promised to, but then I would go out and do it again. So finally, one day in December, I killed two squirrels. Shot them with a double-barreled shotgun down in the bottom of Sweet Gum Hollow. And the burden come on me, People, like it ain't ever done before. Come on me, and I known I had done wrong. It might not be wrong for you'uns to do it or somebody that needed the meat, but it was wrong for me because I was just killing to be killing. So I made a covenant with the Lord that day. I kneeled down right there in the bottom of Sweet Gum Hollow and made a covenant not to never do it no more. But I had the fanger. Yessir, I had the old fanger for killing, and I liked to do it, and I could do it, and I knew before I ever got back home that as long as I had the fanger for it, I wouldn't quit my killing." He raised the nub again.

"So I fixed her."

Pearl closed her eyes, remembering. Margaret looked at her mother, then at Shack's raised hand. She smiled a quick smile.

"I just took an axe and sharpened it up good and laid that fanger up on a log and I fixed her. Like He said to do. 'If thy right hand offend thee, cut if off!' So I whacked her off. I'd do it again, too. I ain't never been sorry I obeyed. And that's what we've got to do, People." He looked at his son.

"We've got to obey the Lord. We can't go letting lust snare us. We gotta do whatever it takes to keep lust from snaring us. We gotta be obedient."

Peeter looked away. His breathing was faster, more difficult. He had a fleeting thought of bright lights outside the movie theater, but he pushed it from his mind.

"We gotta be willing to do whatever it takes," Shack said. "Whatever under the sun that it takes . . ."

Shack started praying, then, and the others bowed their heads. Except Margaret. She stared at Shack, and the smile came again.

Pearl looked at the floor. She did not try to pray. Peeter prayed. Shack's voice roared mightily in the building; he was on his knees.

Suddenly there was a loud thump on the floor, and a shout: "Gawd-a-Mighty!"

The others did not realize at first that it was not Shack who had said it; that it was not Shack stomping the floor. Margaret was the first to know. She caught sight of the body as it fell from the loft through the opening where she had watched the wasps buzzing. But even Margaret did not at first recognize who it was that had fallen. She did not know until after he hit the floor that it was Flank Busby. Then she ran to him.

She lifted his head and held it in her lap and wiped his face with her hand. His face was smeared with dirt and sweat.

"Get away from him!" Shack said. "Get away, Daughter. He's drunk. Get on away. You women folks get on outside."

"He's hurt, Papa," said Margaret.

"He's drunk."

Flank groaned. He looked at Margaret and groaned again.

"He's hurt, Papa," Margaret said. "He's hurt bad."

Flank blinked. "Is this some kinda funeral?" he whispered. He blinked again, then raised up quickly. "Is it mine?" he asked.

#

Chapter 4

Sam Antone Rose lived down the road from Shack. He lived alone and didn't bother anyone. Weeds and grass stunted his crops because Sam did not care for plowing. Some years corn stayed in his fields until February, and the last acre of cotton he raised had hung in the field until wind and rain wrenched it from the bolls and scattered it in the grassy field. Sam raised a few vegetables and a yearling or so each year and a pig or two. And he kept a bull that brought in a little money without much effort on Sam's part. Some people thought Sam was lazy, but they were mistaken. Sam just didn't care.

Sam was small and hard and long-waisted; his belt rode low on his hips so that the cuffs of his trousers were frayed from dragging. Summer and winter he wore a leather billed cap cupped snugly over his small round head.

Shack thought Sam Antone Rose was an agent of the devil. There were several reasons why he thought this. In the first place, Sam didn't look like other people. He had no eyelashes, and his ears lay close to his head as though they were glued on. And he was from somewhere else, nobody seemed to know where. But the real reason Shack didn't like him was because Sam liked grasshoppers. He wouldn't eat them—he wouldn't kill a grasshopper except by accident—but he was crazy about the little hoppers. He would go into the fields and catch jars full of grasshoppers and take them home and turn them loose in his yard. He liked to watch them; he thought there was nothing so beautiful as a grasshopper when it spread its fine wings.

Sam Antone Rose would sit in the grass for hours watching his grasshoppers. He thought it was wonderful the way their tiny jaws cut blades of grass. Watching gave him a feeling of strength and wonder; he liked the perfection, the fine smooth way the little mouths worked and the juice that they made. He liked the spring-like hops of the long legs and the way the bodies moved from the middle backward as they sat still—the fluid-like motion—all of this looked good and beautiful to Sam Antone Rose. Most of all, he liked the thin, clear wings. Sam was thrilled when grasshoppers spread their wings and made short flights. He would hold them and spread their wings gently, carefully, and examine the tissue-fineness, and the perfection.

On the other hand, Shack hated grasshoppers, and he was afraid of them. He connected them with a plague of locusts, which he read about in the Bible, and he had a deep-seated fear that they might some day destroy the world.

Sam watched birds the same way he watched grasshoppers. He especially liked to watch buzzards sailing high, gliding, float-ing, wings spread, and he liked hawks. He studied their wings. He would lie for hours on his back in a pasture to watch circling buz-zards. He had learned a lot this way.

Sam wanted to fly like the lonely buzzards that glided far away on summer days. And some day Sam would fly, too, because in his barn he was building a glider. He had been working on it for a long time. No one else knew except Peeter. He was one of the few visitors Sam had, and he couldn't visit except when Shack was away or when they had a cow to take to Sam's bull.

Despite his odd looks, or perhaps because of them, women loved Sam. He was tender and gentle. But he had never married. He often thought of a family, even sometimes dreamed that he had one, but there was a strange thing in Sam that kept him from getting married. It had been there for a long time, and he had quit having anything to do with women even though they liked him. He did not trust them. You never knew what they were going to do. Like the Widow Lewis, for instance. He had gone with her for two years, walking the three miles to see her several times a week. Then one night he suggested that perhaps they could get married, and the widow went into a rage, threw the quilts back, and yelled until he got up and went home. Since then, Sam had stuck pretty close, catching his grasshoppers, watching buzzards far away, and working on the delicate wings of his glider.

One Saturday afternoon when Shack was in Blue Town castrating pigs, Peeter walked over to Sam Antone Rose's house. He strolled across the front yard and knocked on the door, but no one answered. As he walked around the side of the house, he heard Sam singing: "Always alone. Alone and blue. I've got no one to tell my troubles to." Sam had a fine voice. "Then I awake. And find you gone. It seems that I must always be alone."

Sam was sprawled on the ground with his back against the wall of the house. Sun was shining, and Sam was whittling. Sam watched the tall boy approaching, walking as though he were treading barefoot on broken glass. Peeter's sleeves were down, covering part of his hands. He rubbed his palm across his face and looked away from Sam. He sat beside him.

Now Sam whistled the sad song about being alone. The sun was warm on them. Peeter looked at the thin brown hands. He saw dark bruises on Sam's right knuckles. "What happened to your hand?"

Sam turned the hand up, made a fist, and looked at the greenish purple spots. "Ask that black devil out yonder," he said, meaning the bull that stood beside the barn. He flexed his fingers. "I'll probably have to cut it off."

"How'd you whittle?"

"With one hand."

"What's that you making?"

"Nothing. Dumb little ole hopper."

Peeter knew Sam had many wooden grasshoppers in the house.

A dirty white rooster sidled up. Its tail feathers were gone, and its bottom had a big red bare splotch on it. The rooster pecked at cedar shavings on the ground.

"Git on, Bald Ass," Sam said. "Git!" He didn't much care for chickens because they chased his grasshoppers.

"I got some dandy hoppers this year," he said.

"Yessir, I seen 'em."

"Did?"

"Yessir."

"See there! There goes one. See? Everywhere." He looked at Peeter and blinked the empty lids. "What you been doing, Boy?"

"Nothing. Going to school."

"Learning something?"

Peeter shrugged. "Ain't failing."

"You not going be like me?"

"I don't know," Peeter said. He threw a rock across the yard. "I'll be glad when it's over myself."

"You got a little old gal up there?"

"Nah."

"Huh?"

"Nah."

"I bet you got one."

Peeter didn't say anything. He took a piece of colored glass from his pocket and held it so he could see the sun through it.

"It's your business," said Sam. "A man's girl is his own business, ain't it?"

Peeter twitched his lips and sniffed.

"Keep your eye on 'em though, you hear?"

"Yes sir."

"Why you say 'sir' to me? I ain't nobody. Ain't I told you?"

"Yes sir."

"Well, don't say it no more. Lordamercy, you're bigger'n I am." He started cutting on the wood again, and whistling. He whistled better than anybody else that Peeter knew. The tune was sad, but Peeter liked it. It was the kind of thing he liked to hear sitting in the warm sunshine.

"Old Peete's all right," Sam said. "Going to school all time. Going to be something."

Peeter chewed a blade of grass. Sam scraped his knife blade on the leg of his trousers. "What you going to be?"

Peeter sniffed.

"You not going to be like Sam Antone Rose and do nothing. What you going be?"

"Nothing I don't guess." Peeter jumped and swung on the limb of a tree. With his arms stretched above his head, holding the limb, he faced Sam. "Guess I'll be a mailman or something." He swung again. "Something like that, I reckon."

"Like Mr. Rod?" Sam grinned.

"Might be. I don't know."

"Just ride around all day like Mr. Rod, huh?"

Peeter had thought for a long time that he would like to carry the mail. It had started when he was very small and when Rod Amos would stop his car at their mailbox. Sometimes there was happiness in the box when the car drove away. Sometimes Uncle Frederick sent presents. Or money. You never knew what would be in the box. So very early, Peeter had thought he wanted to be like Mr. Rod and carry happiness to people and now, at sixteen, he knew of nothing better he would like.

"You going to be like Mr. Rod with the women, too?" asked Sam, and Peeter didn't answer. "Better watch out. Better make sure the old man ain't sleeping somewhere or ain't going come sneaking home from the field. Like old Oscar Carter done. Mr. Rod's got some lead in his bony butt right now from Oscar's shotgun. You know that?"

"Uh-uh."

"It's a fact. He thought Oscar was plowing corn, but he wasn't." Sam laughed. "Don't reckon it bothered Mr. Rod none."

Peeter remembered when Ed Bailey's wife quit living with Ed and moved in with Mr. Rod after the mailman's wife died. Peeter heard talk about it, but he hadn't understood it. He never really understood any of the stories he heard about Mr. Rod except that he had a habit of stopping at lonely houses to talk to lonely wives.

"I better go," said Peeter. "Papa'll be home after while."

"Where's he at?"

"Gone working on somebody's hogs."

Sam grinned. He looked across the yard. "Papa the nut-cutter," he said. "How's your mama?"

"All right."

"Your mama's good, huh?"

"Yeah. Papa's good, too. He's all time helping somebody."

"Crazy as a churn full of drunk bumble bees," Sam said.

They sat quietly in the sunshine for awhile. Peeter studied the farm wagon surrounded by grass at the edge of the pasture.

"Who put them rubber tires on that wagon?" Peeter asked.

"Who you think?"

"How come you to?"

"I hated them old rims grinding on rocks," Sam said. "Made my skin crawl." He spat to one side. "My old jalopy blowed up on me, I just switched the wheels."

"How come your bull kicked your hand?" asked Peeter.

"Ah, I lied to you about that."

"He didn't kick you?"

"Nah, I just said that."

"What happened to it?"

"I just said that. It wasn't nothing."

Peeter watched the hands work with the wood. After awhile he stood and stretched. "Want me to draw you some water before I go?"

"You like to."

"I'll draw you some."

Sam watched Peeter walk to the well, noticing the grasshoppers springing into flight as the boy passed, then he looked back at the wood and started whistling the sad song again.

After Peeter left for home, Sam sat a long time in the sunshine, singing: "Nobody's darling on earth. Nobody cares for me. For I am nobody's darling. Nobody cares for me."

He thought of a little boy in another place, a boy named Samuel. It is winter time and the little boy looks out a window at cold, frozen ground and bare empty trees. Then he goes into the kitchen where a fat old woman is cooking. "Mama?" asks the little boy. "Where's Mama?" And the fat old woman, struggling with a clumsy door of an old stove, says angrily: "Don't start that again. I told you she's gone. Mama don't care nothing about you. Ain't I told you? You might as well forget about Mama 'cause she ain't coming back. Go play."

Now Sam quickly got up, put his knife in his pocket, and went inside the house. He stood in his little kitchen and gritted his teeth. He hardened his fist. Quickly, deliberately, he smashed it into the pine boards of the kitchen wall, drew it back and again drove it hard into the wall. Blood came quickly to the surface and covered his knuckles. He walked through the house, humming.

\#

Chapter 5

Flank Busby had been looking for something all his life. Always thin and pale and wormy-looking, he had spent a lot of time alone. Even when he was with people, he always seemed alone. Flank had worked in the field with his brothers and sawed wood and shoveled manure out of cow barns. Summer nights he had sat in darkness with his brothers and neighbor boys, talking until late. But even then the others didn't listen to him. They always listened to his oldest brother Dalt. When Flank told things, his words sort of died, and the others would get quiet for awhile after he quit talking. They seldom laughed or cursed about what he said the way they did when Dalt told something. As he grew older, Flank took to heckling Dalt in a mild, subtle way. He developed a sly sarcasm that while first directed toward Dalt, later dominated his conversations in general.

Flank had a long skinny neck and hair grew down into his collar. His nose was thin, but it was sunken in the middle as though it had been struck with a two-by-four, and you had to look twice to see the pale thin lips. His hair was fine and thin, his little round eyes stuck deep in his face. Flank writhed rather than walked. He slunk as you would expect a skinny person with a long slender neck and small round eyes to slink. He had never in his life walked erect. He talked as though he had just been crying.

It was true that Flank drank more than he should, and his drinking had caused the captain of the last destroyer he was on to break him to seaman shortly before his discharge. It hadn't made any difference to Flank. He had never felt like he was much good anyway. He had grown up feeling this way. He was Joe Busby's third son, but Joe didn't claim him. Joe always accused his wife—herself a Holiness preacher of a sort—of being unfaithful with a visiting evangelist the summer before Flank was born. Flank learned about this when he was very young. Joe yelled it at him in a cornfield one day. After that, Flank knew it more by what Joe didn't say to him than by what he said. He just didn't say much of anything to Flank. He fussed with the others, but he didn't even do this with Flank. He treated him the way he would have treated a daughter if he'd had one. (It was because of Joe, who could not pronounce his "r"s, that Frank Busby became "Flank".)

Flank's hair was red while his brothers had black hair like their mother and father. Flank's mother had been a huge, plump woman. Most of the time she didn't preach, but she played her part in the pews. She drew attention like a spotlight. Seated midway of the congregation, she would begin with a low groan—lips barely open, broad fat face tilted slightly. "Aye-men! Aaaye-men!"

It would come from the deep pool of her throat like marvelous bubbles rising to the top in a pond. And when children would stare at her, craning their necks, turning to find the source of the low growl-groan, she would roll her great yellow eyes at them. The eyes, huge in her bronze face, were frightening but they did not roll wildly; they were controlled, focusing quietly on each of the curious ones so that the children would quickly turn away.

The eyes sat high and alone in the face, like two cats perched on high limbs, detached from and superior to the deep voice. The eyes both guarded the voice, pampered and indulged it, and also ridiculed it. So that when you saw the eyes, you thought one second they were going to join the snickering boys in laughing at the voice and the next that they were going to strike dead anyone who dared laugh.

This was Flank's mother. Her gray-streaked hair was swept up like sedge grass into long waving stands, wet with oil. And as the preacher built up steam, Sister Busby would accompany him like an organ: "Aye-Men! Glory to God. Hallelujah! Aye-Men!" Rising loudly so that even the preacher's voice could not be heard and at other times dropping to a hoarse whisper, and all the time her great amber eyes were rolling from side to side, studying, analyzing every response, warning, pampering.

She also prayed at home. Flank, racing through the house, running from room to room, often stumbled over her as she knelt on the floor praying. She would never stop praying because of these interruptions. Sometimes she would pop him with an open palm, but she wouldn't stop praying. Rather, the collisions always set her off, growling and groaning in the low deep way.

Sister Busby died while Flank was shacked up with a whore in Japan. He didn't know she was dead until two days after. The telegram was waiting when he got back to the ship. That was the last time Flank had messed with a woman.

Now he was home again, and things had not changed between him and Joe. He still had no father, and now he didn't have a mother, either. So Flank stayed drunk most of the time. But he was still looking for something.

He couldn't forget Margaret. He kept remembering the way she had looked the morning he fell from the church loft. It hadn't hurt him seriously—knocked the breath out of him and sprained his shoulder. But it had scared him, and for an instant he had thought he had passed from life to death and that Margaret was a freckled-faced angel. Just as quickly, Shack had become the devil, ordering him out of the building, condemning him.

Flank had left, but he felt he had as much claim to the old school house as did Shack. He had slept there many nights, sometimes on the floor, sometimes on the hard benches, and sometimes in the attic. Old draperies were piled up there, and on cool nights, he had covered with these.

On an afternoon in May, after spending a drunken night in the old building, Flank felt depressed and went for a walk in the sunshine. He had a feeling that he was going to die. Such feelings were not new to him; he was always getting premonitions. He walked slowly, head lowered, and thought about how it would be if he should die. He pictured Joe receiving the news and being stunned with grief. He thought of his casket in the living room of the old Busby house, sitting in the same place where they said his mother's had been. His cousin, Agnes Ferguson, had made pictures of the casket and of Sister Busby in it and kept them to show to Flank when he came home. He thought of Dalt and Albert Lee and Agnes and all the others sitting in the room, around the casket, crying and carrying on about "Little Flank." Or maybe they wouldn't cry. Maybe Joe would be happy that his bastard son was dead. Flank wondered who would preach his funeral, whether any preacher would stoop to such a chore.

"By Grannies," he said aloud. "I'll bet old Shack would."

He had wound his way onto a railroad track and was almost to a trestle that crossed a small gravel pit filled with water. Shack would preach his funeral there in the old school house, and Margaret, the girl with the freckled angel face, would be there, and she would cry for him.

Flank sat on the edge of the trestle and dangled his feet over the side. A man and two young boys were fishing. The sun was behind the trees, and shadows were purple in the water. Flank did not know the people. The boy on the far side caught a small sun perch. The other boy yelled at him: "Dadgumit, Roy, you ain't supposed to catch 'em all."

"Gitting me a mess."

"Liable to founder yourself," the man said. He looked up at Flank and grinned.

"They biting?" asked Flank.

"Frigging gnats are."

A frog croaked in the bushes, and the weeds on the other side sang with crickets. It made Flank sad. He thought about Joe Busby. He wondered if Joe was really his father. He didn't think so. He didn't believe his mother had been unfaithful to Joe, yet he didn't think he was Joe's son. He accepted both beliefs. Often he wondered what the evangelist had looked like. Sometimes he couldn't sleep at night for thinking about it and wondering about the man. It was like trying to remember when you were a baby, or looking for a footprint after a heavy rain. Somewhere there had been a father—somewhere there was a father—and he would never know him.

"Hell, got my bait," the larger kid said.

"You cut out that cussing, Roy," the man said.

"Cal cusses."

"It don't make a nevermine what Cal done. I said you cut it out."

"Shit," Roy said quietly.

The man looked at Flank. "You got a smoke?"

"No," said Flank.

The man took a plug of tobacco from his pocket and bit off a chew.

"Give me some of that, Daddy," Cal said, and the man passed it to him.

"Thow me some," called Roy.

"You don't need none," the man said. He looked again at Flank. "Ain't I seen you?" he asked.

"I don't know, I been standing up here about ten minutes," Flank said with a snicker. A kingfisher passed over quickly, dipped into the water, and flew away.

"Ain't you Sister Busby's boy?"

"What's left of him," Flank said.

"That's what I thought." He pulled his hook in, stuck another worm on it, and threw it back into the water. "You religious like she is?"

"I didn't get much of a dose," Flank said.

"She's got a heap of it," the man said. "I never seen nobody talk the tongues like she does. I've heered her preach. She tried to save me one time."

He took another chew of tobacco and squatted. "She can talk them tongues. I belief if I'd ever gone back and heered her one more time, she woulda saved me. Hell, I don't know."

Flank didn't say anything.

"How's she getting along?"

Flank didn't answer.

"I say how's Sister Busby getting along?"

"She's died."

"Aw." He stared at Flank. "I didn't know she died. You sure?"

"She died December year ago."

The man stood silently, holding his pole. "I didn't know it. I'll be dadblamed. She sure as God could talk them tongues. I belief she woulda saved me if I'd gone back one more time."

Flank sat quietly, watching it get dark, and thought of the big plump woman with the amber eyes. He wanted to go talk to her, but there was nowhere to go. She was dead. Like the day was dying now. Flank remembered nights when he had gone to church with her and slept on the benches with his head in her lap. He thought of all the sweet-smelling Japanese women he'd messed with and wished they weren't true, and of the whisky that Sister Busby hated so, and he wanted to go home and to talk to her and to promise never to get drunk again. But Sister Busby was dead.

Tears ran down Flank's face as the fishers went away from the darkening pit. He sat alone, listening to the night birds and the frogs, and his arms grew cold.

This was the trestle where Shack almost got run over by a train. It was where Hoyt Mitchell had been killed. Right over there. He knew exactly where the wheels had sliced through Hoyt's body.

It happened when Flank was a little boy. Hoyt and Shack were on the trestle, drunk, late one night. Nobody knew why they were there, but they were lying on the trestle when a train came. Shack managed to dangle from the end of a crosstie while the train roared by, but Hoyt didn't make it, and Shack saw part of him fall into the water. Hoyt's blood had splattered Shack's face. They said this was when Shack changed.

It seemed strange to Flank now, thinking of where Hoyt had died. Right over there. In the dark. He could almost hear the splash.

Flank liked Shack. He was a strong man. And a good man, too. Flank sat in the darkness thinking about what a good man Shack was. And about the girl with the angel face.

#

Chapter 6

They said money was hidden in the woods near Scuppernong. Years before, around 1910, the bank at Whitt City had been robbed. Some said three men went into the bank while one stood on the street, and others, when they told it now, said only two entered the bank. However many robbers participated, two men were shot and killed in the noon-day robbery. The banker—old man Quince Whitt—was shot in the back after he panicked and ran toward the door. And a one-armed deputy sheriff, Billy Lee Mitchum, was shot to death in the street as the robbers fled.

Later that week three strange horsemen—one said to have been an Indian—were seen riding into the woods near Scuppernong. Three days later, two horsemen rode out. Folks who saw them said there had been sacks on the horses when they entered the woods, but the bags were missing when the two horsemen rode away.

A lot of people had searched in the years since the robbery, but the money had never been found. Now most everyone had forgotten it, save a few old timers who talked about it over campfires during coon hunts and fishing trips.

The storied woods were on Carlton Logan's farm, and he knew the story well. He hoped to find the money, and after nearly forty years he still looked for it. Logan wouldn't allow anybody to hunt on his land. He had, hidden in his barn, maps that he had drawn, outlining sections of the woods with places marked where he planned to dig. He was getting old, and it haunted him that he might never find the treasure. He lay awake nights thinking about it, tracing in his mind paths that wound through his woods, remembering rocks and boulders and stumps and plotting new places to search.

Now that he was growing old, Logan thought about getting someone to join him in the search. He wished there was someone with whom he could share his knowledge and hunches, but he didn't know of a single person whom he could trust. He especially did not trust Norm Otwell, a younger man who had bought the adjoining farm. Norm had often mentioned the stories of the buried treasure to Logan, saying, "We oughta go in there and find that stuff."

Logan had discouraged any such talk, dismissing it as "a lot of hooey." But Logan knew it was true. He had evidence in the loft of his barn. In a box, under a pile of hay in his barn loft, Logan had the skeleton of a man whom he was convinced was the third strange horseman. He had hidden the bones there for fifteen years. No one else, not even his wife Effie—who, had she known, would have told everybody in the county—knew about the skeleton.

Logan had found the bones by accident one day when he wasn't even searching for the treasure—at least his search had been secondary; he was always searching. He had gone into the woods looking for a lost calf and sat on a boulder to rest. A large vine, growing from under the stone and across it, made him uncomfortable, and when he pulled it loose, he noticed a peculiar softness in the ground. Rolling the stone aside, he found the bones in a leaf-covered hollow. A small hole was in the center of the skull. With the bones, Logan had found a rusted, pearl-handled revolver. It was in the box with the bones now under hay in Logan's barn loft.

There had been other discoveries. Not far from where he discovered the skeleton, Logan found a small hole drilled in a rock and filled with lead. Marks were cut into a huge tree in the area, too. So Logan thought he knew about where the money was, but he had never found it.

Norm Otwell's well had gone dry that spring. Drillers had tried twice, unsuccessfully, to find water, and someone suggested that a water witcher be brought in to advise the drillers. Shack, having a reputation as the most dependable witcher in the county, was contacted and promised to locate water.

Several men were at the farm when Shack arrived. He wore his long white coat, black lace-boots, a black string-tie and white hat. He placed a box on the ground near the driller's rig. He barely spoke and appeared deep in thought. He walked away from the site to the top of a small hill and sat alone.

Shack didn't charge to witch water. It was a way he could be of service, and he took pleasure in it. It was another of the powers that had been given him, and he was grateful. He thought of witching as one of the talents with which he had been entrusted, and he wanted to be a faithful steward.

Shack felt good about this day. He wanted to take it slow and savor the goodness. He felt close to the knot of men waiting for him to perform. Cattle grazed in a nearby pasture. Shack looked at them, recognizing some of the fat young steers as ones that he had cut for Logan. That was another talent of which he was proud. Shack liked the steers. He liked them better than the bulls. He thought of steers as being pure—selected and set apart to become fat and sleek and to furnish good, pure meat. He thought of them as being clean and undefiled, and he had played a part in it. Shack wished the men down there also could be undefiled—that he, by so simple an act, could make them so. He wished that he could make all men pure and clean. O God, that he could! But he could not. There was so little he could do. It caused a dark shadow in Shack's mind and on the day. There was so much impurity in the world, and he was powerless against it, even in his own home. But the Lord would provide. He would trust the Lord to show him what to do about keeping his own family pure.

Shack went to where the men waited and removed a large black cloth from the box and spread it on the ground. He took from the box a small tin bucket, painted black on the outside. A piece of cord dangled from the pail's bottom, and a heavy nail was tied to the string. Shack took off his coat, folded it carefully, and placed it on the ground. He put his hat on top of it and rolled his sleeves above his elbows. He studied the area closely and stepped off the distance between the two dry holes. Shack stretched out his hand, palm down, and turned in a half-circle. No one said anything. Then he spread the black cloth over his head. It reached to his waist. He took the bucket under the cloth with him so that only the nail and string could be seen. Slowly Shack moved over the ground. The string and nail swung back and forth. Occasionally Shack stopped, and the string continued swinging.

"Most generally, witchers use a peach limb," Alex Gardner said.

"Shack don't use no limb," another man said. "He uses that little box. Finds water, too. I seen him once over at Blue Town. Old Buster Cooper had drilled holes all over the place. You couldn't walk without stepping in a hole, and he hadn't got a drop of water. I mean nothing, Buddy, and they got ahold of old Shack, and he come out there like he's doing here and witched it. Buddy, he told 'em right where to dig, and they didn't want to do it. Hi Jones had his rig out there, and he said no sir, he wasn't going to waste time drilling that close to where he'd hit a dry hole. I mean there wasn't a drop, Buddy. And old Shack said, 'Well, you drill anyhow, Mister Jones, and if you don't get water at eighty-five foot, I'll pay for all your trouble' and Buddy he done it. Hit the best stream of water you ever seen at eighty-two foot I believe it was. He don't need no peach limb, Shack don't."

Shack was moving slowly now. Suddenly he stopped altogether and began to tremble and shake beneath the cloth. His knees buckled, and he fell to the ground so that only a black bundle of cloth showed. Then he yelled, a shrill cry: "Here! Here!" He came off the ground, slung the cloth away, and looked happily at the men who stood quietly watching.

"I found it!" he announced. He pulled a small stake from his pocket, stuck it in the ground and hammered it with his boot heel. "There's your water, Norm," he said. "Go down sixty-five foot, and you'll get all the water a body could want." He turned to face Norm again. "More than you will ever need," he added softly.

Afterward, before Shack left, the men gathered around where he sat on a nearby knoll and questioned him about witching.

"It's a gift of the Lord," Shack explained. "You see, down in the ground is just like blood vessels in a man's leg. All them streams winding in and around, twisting here and there like blood vessels, and with the power, you can see them. That's what I do—I see them. Just like I see other things. 'He who has eyes to see, let him see.' It's a gift, People."

"What part does the bucket play?" asked Alex. "First time I ever seen a bucket. All I ever seen before was peach limbs."

"Bucket's just my instrument," Shack said. "Limbs are the same thing. Just instruments. The power's the thing." He looked around. Carlton Logan was watching him closely.

"And I'm just a instrument," Shack said. "Just a instrument in the hands of the Lord."

He was silent a minute. "You can be that, too, men. Everyone of you can be a instrument in the hand of the Lord if you will." He looked away. "But you won't," he added quietly. "You won't yield yourself. That's why He'll destroy you." He stood. He had his coat on now, and he put his hat on, too. "That's why He's going to destroy it all pretty soon."

"Is the world coming to an end?"

Shack looked at the man who had asked. He nodded.

"When?" several asked.

Shack smiled. "You'll know in due time," he said. He looked at the sky and raised a hand toward the heavens. "I see things," he said. He looked into the men's faces. "I see things, just like I seen water in the ground." He stared from one face to another. "And I see things in you," he added. His gaze stopped on Carlton Logan, and the old man shifted.

"I see things," Shack said quietly. He held Logan's gaze an instant longer, then turned to Norm Otwell.

"I found you water, Norm," he said. "I found you water like I said I would. But . . ." He looked at the ground, then back to Norm. "You want to hear it? You want to know what I see?"

"I reckon so, Shack." Norm laughed.

"I found you water, Norm. Good, cold water. Drink it while the sun is warm, Norm, because when the frost is on the vine, it'll be too late. When the frost is on the vine, you'll drink only at the spring eternal."

The men were quiet. Norm cleared his throat. "Well, I reckon we'll have to wait a day or so to know if you've found the water," he said.

Shack looked at him, but it was as though he looked through him. "Wood and stone," Shack said softly. "The wood and the stone will come before the frost is on the vine. And after that, the spring eternal."

"Hell," Norm whispered and laughed.

Shack moved among the men and stopped beside Carlton Logan. He rested a hand on the old man's shoulder. "There is a secret in this man," Shack said. "There is a secret buried deep in this man—hidden like water in the ground. There is a secret here."

Logan wiped his mouth on his sleeve.

Shack looked at other faces, then he placed his other hand on Logan. "The everlasting grin," he said, looking straight into Logan's eyes. "In a high place there is an everlasting grin."

Logan did not move, but his face turned pale.

Shack walked quickly off the knoll, toward the tree where his horse was tied. Carlton Logan took a step away from the crowd. "Wait, Mister," he called. "Wait, now!"

But Shack was already riding away on the roan-colored horse.

#

Chapter 7

Wasps hummed in the old Sutton School, circled in the dark air, and finally clung upside down on a gray nest in the corner of the ceiling. Flank Busby lay on a bench watching. He saw them fly and come back again. It was very hot inside.

Flank had gone home the previous night. The house was different when he thought about it now. He was already missing it. He tried to think of how it actually was; tried to remember the room and the cot where he had slept. There was something there when he was away from it that he always wanted to go back and find, but when he went back, it was never there. And when he was back, he couldn't remember how he had felt while away, so that the good of being there was lost. It was the same way with thinking of his brothers and of Joe Busby.

He had thought of them that week and wanted to go home and talk with them, but when he got there, it had all changed. When he tried to say the things he had thought he would say, he no longer even wanted to say them, and he couldn't say them, and so the sullenness, the stiffness, had returned to his own throat as soon as he was with them. By Saturday morning the stiffness in him and in Joe, in all of them, had evolved into bitterness, and before they were through with breakfast, he was yelling at Joe Busby and Joe was staring out the window, sitting cross-legged at the table, chewing and talking, saying: "When'd you ever hope me any?" Sucking air through his teeth and jerking his lip. "How much corn you plowed this year? You seen him plow any, Dalt?"

Sucking air again and laughing, then looking across the table, that long cold look from that far-away place, then staring out the window again and making another sucking noise somewhere inside his mouth. "Could used him busting them middles. That right, Dalt? You could hoped Dalt. Ain't never hoped nobody."

The wasps got in each other's way and one flew off, came back, touched the nest, left it, came again and settled. Flank got up and peered through a window. He went to the door and looked at the road. With a handkerchief he wiped sweat off his chest and arms. He smoked a cigarette.

Wild pink roses ran along a rusty fence outside. Dust lay thick on the leaves. Flank looked at the dirty floor. Bits of paper, tangled in balls of dust, lay under the benches. Old rags, used for dusting in days past, lay in a corner. Flank lay down again and watched the wasps. The baby wasps would be good fish bait. He thought of the two boys and their father fishing in the late evening, and of what the man had said about Sister Busby: "She sure as God could talk them tongues."

Flank thought of the late dark evenings of another time, before the lamps were lighted, when he had stumbled on his mother, kneeling in the house. Lying on the cot the night before, he had thought of her and, during the night, while Joe Busby snored somewhere, he had wanted to walk through the dark rooms and stumble on his mother again.

Flank heard a dirt-dauber humming in a mud tunnel under one of the benches. He lay very still and very quiet and watched the wasps and listened to the dirt-dauber. I don't care, he thought. I'll just lay here. Could fish. Go down there. Ah no. Don't want to. No pole nohow. I'll just lay here. Then what? It's the then-whats that get you. Always got to do something then do something else. What's the use of doing any of it, but what happens if you don't? Couldn't drink enough to keep you drunk even if you had enough of it. If you could just stay drunk. Stay somewhere down there in the bottom of it so you didn't know about the then-whats, but even there you know something and when you finally see that you can't get away, you float back to the top, and there's always the hole inside you because you're by yourself, and you don't know where you come from or what to do about it or what to do or not do. About anything.

Wish I could talk the tongues. Or something. Like *she* done. She knowed something out there. Somewheres. I reckon. All that praying. Wish I felt it like she did. Or something.

Dear Heavenly Father. Thou knowest that I ah Thou canst heal. Grant Heavenly Father. Grant. Grant. She said grant a lot. Dear Heavenly Father. Shoot. I can't do nothing. Just talk to myself. I'll just lay here by God and tonight go to Aunt Tessie's and then what? To hell with then what.

Later, when he awoke in the hot stickiness, he saw the girl with the angel face not ten feet away. He lay still and looked at her. Finally he sat and scratched the back of his neck and kept looking at her.

"I didn't know nobody was here," Margaret said. She started searching the other benches.

"What you lost?"

"My purse. Left it here the other day."

"I ain't seen it."

"I betcha it's gone." She kept looking as Flank watched. "Didn't know nobody was here."

"I been sleep," said Flank. "I ain't seen your purse." He lighted a cigarette.

When she had searched the room, Margaret came near him. "What you gawking at?"

"Nothing."

"You thinking how ugly I am, I already know that."

"Nah, I wasn't thinking that, Margaret."

"I didn't know you'd be here, or I wouldn't come."

"I'm glad you come," he said.

She stooped to look under a bench—searching for something she knew wasn't there.

"I been lonesome as a three-day-old cat," Flank said. "You ever get lonesome, Hon?"

"I wonder where that dumb purse is at."

"I just been laying here thinking about how the whole world is lonesome. Them trees are lonesome. And them roses. Everything is lonesome. It don't make no difference where you go, it's still lonesome. It was lonesome in Japan. I bet you're lonesome."

"Ain't got no time to be lonesome," she said.

"I been lonesome all day long," Flank said. "Even when I go to sleep, I get lonesome. Specially when I first wake up."

She wasn't looking at him, but she wasn't looking for the purse either. She faced the door.

"You make that dress?"

"Ain't a dress. It's a skirt."

"Whatever it is, it's pretty."

"I ain't got time to get lonesome, sewing and all. Arning."

"How come you up here?"

"I told you."

"You been fussing with your mammy?"

Margaret looked his way. "I didn't know it was nobody here."

"You didn't know it was nobody up in that attic that day neither." He snickered.

She looked at the hole in the ceiling.

"Say, you didn't know old Flank was up in that hole, did you?" He laughed, and Margaret started laughing, too.

"Huh? You didn't, did you? I bet you thought the roof was caving in, didn't you?" They both laughed, almost hysterically.

"I thought you'd killed yourself," she said.

"How come you to run up to me like that?"

"I thought you was hurt."

Flank went closer and tried to put his arms around her, but she pulled away.

"Aw, I didn't mean nothing, Marg. Shoot. I didn't . . . don't you get mad at me now." He turned away. "There's a dirt-dauber under there somewheres."

"They won't sting you."

"One stung Dalt one time."

"They won't sting you," Margaret said.

"One stung Dalt, and Mama put snuff on it. We used to knock down wasp nests. Onc't me and Dalt was knocking one down, and I got stung on the eye and couldn't see nothing for two, three days. We had a dog. I didn't know you then, Margaret. We had a dog, and he didn't have no tail, and we called him Turk."

"I gotta go," she said.

"How come? I ain't going to hurt you none."

"Papa'd kill me if he caught me up here with you."

"He don't like me, does he?"

"He don't like no boy," said Margaret. "Not none that I like."

"I like you, Margaret," Flank said.

"Papa told me that day after you fell that I better not ever be seeing you."

"Aw, Shack don't mean it," Flank said.

"Does, too. You don't know Papa. You don't know how he is about me talking to boys."

"He ought not do you that way."

"He's mean."

"Aw, Shack's not mean. He just talks mean."

Margaret leaned closer. "He's mean as a rattlesnake."

"Aw."

"Tell me! He liked to have killed me for running up to you after you fell. You don't know him. Nobody knows him the way I do." Words poured from her now, and Flank perched on the back of a bench, listening.

"I'll tell you something if you won't tell nobody," said Margaret.

"What?"

"You better not never tell on me."

"I won't never."

"I tried to kill Papa one time."

"Aw, shoot, Margaret. You never done it."

"I liked to have poisoned him," she said and giggled. "Don't you never tell."

"You ought not talk like that," Flank said. "Your papa's a good old boy."

"I put rat poison in his cornbread," Margaret said. "You know what he said? Just me and him—Mama was sick—and I put some of it in Papa's bread. It was real white-like. You know what he said? Wye, just smacked his lips and said 'Sister'—you know how he talks—'Sister,' he says, 'this is the best cornbread I ever et.' And he started crumbling the stuff into his sweet milk and it full of rat poison. I figured—don't you never dare tell none of this—I figured he just about had enough in his belly to kill a mule and him still crumbling up more in his milk. And I didn't care how much of it he eat, but then Peeter come home and Papa told him how good the cornbread was and said 'Get you a chunk of this corn-bread, Son.' Said 'Sister's made up some pretty good cornbread.' And Peeter, little fool, started over to get him a piece of it, and I jumped up and yelled at him to not touch it, and I grabbed ahold of what was left of the cornbread in the skillet and said, 'Why don't y'all shut up about this old cornbread? I know it ain't fit to eat,' and I run to the back door and thowed it out in the yard, and Papa didn't like that.

"This old dog Peeter had—called him Rebecca Anne—he come a running and snatched up that bread and run off with it. Next morning that dog was stone-cold dead as a coot. You know what Papa said when he got up? Come in the kitchen next morning, old fool, and looked around and belched kinda and said, 'I got heartburn from something you cooked last night, Sister.' Called it heartburn. Don't you never tell nobody about that."

"I won't," Flank whispered reverently. He kept looking at her. Then he looked at the floor and laughed. "You beat all I ever seen." He lighted another cigarette.

"Said 'Sister, I want to tell you something'—he's always wanting to tell somebody something. I get sick and tired of him all time going to tell somebody something. Said 'I want to tell you something for your own good. It won't do for you to be seeing that Busby boy.' You oughta heard what he said about you. Said the Devil put you up in that loft." She cackled loudly and slapped her hands together. "Did you know the Devil's the one who done that? Way he talked, I reckon you and the Devil must be good buddies. Said if I ever messed with you, something bad would happen to me sure."

Flank snickered and wiped his forehead on his arm. He wished he could quit sweating. "What'd he say would happen?"

"Heck, I don't know. Lightning'll strike us both, I reckon. That's what he usually says will happen. He ain't got no sense."

Flank put his arm around Margaret. She jerked away, and her hand knocked his cigarette out of his mouth. He caught her and put his arms around her again and kissed her. She turned her head away. "I'm too ugly!"

"No you ain't! Honest, Sweetheart, you ain't. You pretty."

She let him kiss her again. She lay her head against his chest. "You not bad," she whispered. "I don't care what Papa says. You ain't no bad boy."

"I'm going to come see you."

"I wish you could."

"I am."

"I wish Papa would let you," she said. "Like other folks."

"I'm going to come see you and eat supper with you."

"I'll make you a shirt," she said.

"I been lonesome all day," Flank said.

"You lonesome now?"

"No I ain't."

"I been lonesome all my life," Margaret said.

"I ain't going let you be lonesome no more."

"You know something? Don't never tell nobody, but I didn't lose no purse."

"Aw!"

"Nah. You know why I come up here? I come just on account of I wanted to see you. And you was right. Me and Mama did have a fuss. You was right about that. And I told her I was going to run off, but she didn't believe me, and she don't know where I'm at."

"You beautiful!" Flank said.

Margaret turned her face so he could kiss her, but instead, he bolted away.

"What's wrong?"

"The dern house is on far!" Flank cried.

Then Margaret saw great orange wiggling flames running up the wall and smoke boiling toward her.

"Lordy!" she cried. The fire was spreading fast in the old wood, and flames were reaching into the aisle, blocking the door.

"We can't get out," she said. "What we going to do, Flank?"

But Flank was on his way out, going head-first through a screenless window. He hit the ground and started running. He turned and saw Margaret crawling through the window.

"Wait on me!" she called.

"Run, Girl!" Flank cried.

#

Chapter 8

Peeter was thinning corn when he first saw the girl He leaned on the hoe handle, looking, then he scraped the dry dirt again, clipping tender corn sprouts and weeds as he shaved the surface of the ridge, leaving the other corn plants clean by themselves, spaced with enough room to grow.

He watched her come away from the trees, across the rows. Her knees showed when she stepped across the corn rows; the print dress moved carelessly, lightly, as though it would easily blow away. She stopped in the low middle between rows. Peeter saw the ragged canvas shoes, spread wide apart, coated with dust. She wasn't tall. She moved some hair away from her cheek and squinted at him. "Hey," she said. Her hands were on her hips.

Peeter cleared his throat. He saw the hem of her dress move slightly, like the blades of corn. He chopped another sprout.

"You working hard?"

Peeter twitched his lips to one side and sniffed. "Nah," he said, clearing his throat. He looked at the face, brown like her legs. "Thinning corn," he said. He scratched the ground lightly and twitched his lips again.

"My name's Lily," she said. "We're going to live over there close to y'all." Peeter didn't say anything. "I guess so, anyway," she added. "Y'all live in that house over yonder, don't you?" The house was not in sight.

"Yeah," Peeter said. "I seen y'all moving in."

"Lord goodness, it took us all day long."

"What's your last name?"

"Partin." She snickered. "Ain't that a name! Lily Partin went a . . . I better not finish it."

Peeter started to speak but didn't. The print dress was loose, flimsy. It was dark gray spotted with small purple flowers, and white buttons were on the front. Peeter felt kind of sick.

"My daddy just got out of the pen," she said.

"How come?"

"Cause he got caught."

"Oh."

"They busted his still and everything."

Her eyes were very dark, but he couldn't see them well because of the way she squinted.

"Don't say nothing about it," she said. "They don't want no-body to know it."

"All right."

"You won't, will you?"

"Nah."

"I don't care myself, but they do. What's your name?"

"Peeter."

He heard her quick snicker and thought she would make a vul-gar joke like boys did sometimes at school.

"Old Pete," she said.

He moved the hoe.

Lily squatted in the row; her knees broadened toward him. She wiped the hair off her forehead. "This all your land?"

"Papa's."

"Shack?"

Peeter nodded.

"I heard about Shack," she said.

"It's not his," Peeter corrected. "We just work it. I meant." He leaned on the hoe handle. "What grade you in?"

"Seventh. I failed. Flat out, tee-totally flunked-tee-do. I may not go back. No sense in it."

One button was missing on the front, and Peeter saw a bit of white cloth there.

"Who you go with?" she asked.

He cleared his throat. "Nobody."

"Shoot!"

He scraped at the dry dirt. The hoe grated against a rock.

"I don't go with nobody," she said. "Not right now at this very minute nohow. Course I don't know nobody. But you. I have went with somebody, but I don't right now. I bet you do, though."

"No I don't."

She scooped a handful of soft dirt and let it sift through her fist onto the ground. She staggered slightly, almost losing her balance on the uneven ground.

"Lordamercy! I'll stomp your gol-derned corn plumb down." She giggled. "Then old Peeter wouldn't have to hoe it."

Peeter laughed, too. The print dress was moving carelessly, like a fern underwater. Lily wiped her dusty hand on it. Peeter wanted to touch her.

Lily jumped flat-foot across the corn. Her back was toward him. She jumped again—legs springing, bouncing—across another row, and he saw a flutter of white. She almost fell and turned toward him, laughing. "Old Peeter," she said. "Anybody call you Pete?"

He shook his head.

"Well, I might!"

He felt helpless and sort of weak and couldn't stand to look at the brown, wide-spread legs anymore or at the bare ankles turned sideways in loose dirt, but he couldn't *not* look either. The world had stopped, and the part of the cornfield where they stood was suddenly like a hilltop, and he and Lily were giants, and he couldn't see or hear anything outside that circle. It was as though the trees beyond Lily were no bigger than the tiny blades of corn, and everything beyond their plot of loose dirt was blurred. He thought that she must know about his ripe feeling, and he wanted at once to hide it from her and to share it.

"You sick at your stomach?" she asked.

Peeter shook his head. The world was ending. Action was inevitable, but he didn't know how to start it; he was waiting for whatever would happen to happen. There was only the brown body under the loose print dress, and black squinting eyes, and blowing black hair, and missing button. He leaned heavily on the hoe handle. Then he heard approaching footsteps loud like the only noise in the world, and he knew that it was Shack.

Awkwardly, stiffly, he whacked the hoe into the ground; frantically, he tore into the weeded ridge of the corn row. Lily turned her squinting wrinkled-nose face toward the tall man with a rose in his coat. He stared at her.

"Hey," she said.

He didn't answer. He stopped in front of Peeter, between him and Lily, and looked hard into the boy's face. Peeter glanced once. Shack's eyes had changed color.

"What do you think you're doing?" Shack asked between clenched teeth. His great hand trembled as it pawed at the lapel of his coat. The nub of his index finger was lifted slightly, protected from contact. "What are you doing?"

Peeter twitched his lip and sniffed. "Hoeing," he said. He bent over the row. The warm, ripe feeling had flown, and Shack stood, staring. The world was smaller, and there was only one giant in it. But the hoe was big and heavy, and Peeter's hands felt huge as he fought the weeds. The voice of Lily Partin was as strange as wind in the trees, saying, "Shoot, Peeter, I got to go to the house. I guess Mama wonders where I'm at."

Then there was just Shack's heavy breathing, and Peeter was afraid to even think of the brown legs hopping over tender green corn. Shack moved with him, keeping abreast of him. The scraping of the hoe was loud, sometimes it struck stone or sloughed in the dirt, and when finally Shack spoke, his voice was loud in the field: "Her end is rotten as wormwood," he said.

Peeter looked away, toward the woods.

"The end of the evil woman is like rotten wormwood."

Shack grabbed Peeter's shoulders, gripping them strongly with his big hurting fingers. "Do you hear me, Boy?" he demanded. "Do you hear what I say?"

Peeter touched the back of his neck and twitched his lips to one side. He nodded.

"Do you hear me?" Shack gripped hard and shook him. "Do you?"

"Yes sir." Peeter dropped the hoe handle and slipped his hands into his pockets. His fingers found a small round piece of slick glass. He clasped it tightly. It was dark purple, he knew, and he thought sickly of the tiny purple flowers on Lily's dress.

"Say something!" Shack said. "Say something, do you hear me?"

Tears rolled out of Peeter's eyes. Shack held the shoulders an instant longer then turned loose. He walked away, looking down.

"Lord, God forgive him!" he said.

Peeter picked up the hoe and started down the row again. He knew Shack was talking, or praying, or something, but he didn't know what else he said. He didn't hear anything but the "sluff-sluff" of the hoe and the occasional grating of the metal blade against stone.

Chapter 9

Five people and a dog were on the courthouse lawn at Whitt City, and none of these paid any attention to Shack when he first got there. The dog, unaware that his father had been one of the best bird dogs in the county or that his mother was shot for sucking eggs, lay under a bush where he spent most of every day in defiance of a city ordinance and untagged in flagrant violation of state law. He would, if anybody stopped to think about it, never amount to anything. He was just a brown and white smear on the courthouse lawn.

Mrs. Edna Marie Ophelia Brown was sitting on a bench with two of her kids. She was by profession a prostitute. Being a member of no union, her wages were low and varied from a sack of Irish potatoes to a five-dollar bill, depending upon the amount of raw whisky her clients drank, the time of week (whether it was close to payday), and whether they were her friends, her cousins, or new in town.

It was too early to go to the joints, too early to go home; it was a time for sitting and watching to see who came to town. She liked to see what the wives looked like.

"Mama, can I go to Sunday school tomorrow?" asked her little boy, who was lying on his belly across the cement bench. He asked again before she answered: "If Mama feels like it."

"Sunny cool," said the smaller boy, dressed in diapers and sitting on the ground with both fists full of grass.

"Hey Red!" cried one of the other inhabitants of the lawn. "Hey Red!" There was nobody around named "Red," and nobody answered, but still, from time to time, the fat boy in overalls stood and yelled, "Hey Red!" He always did that. He didn't know any better.

The other person was blind. He sat on the steps of the court-house playing a guitar and selling shopping bags. He had never seen a thing in all his life; he didn't even know what the word "see" meant. There had always been a great black spot somewhere, and he was at the center of it. He had never seen light. He remembered a long time back when his mother would hold something in front of him and say, "See this, Art? You see this here match?" And sometimes he would feel some little warm tickle against his face, like a tiny breeze, but he could never see what she wanted him to see. Had he been born without hands, he might never have known that he was solid and not just part of a black circle. He smelled the grass and knew it had been mowed. He smelled old varnish on his guitar; he smelled a cigar that somebody had thrown near the sidewalk, and he smelled the sweet scent of the bushes. These were things that came into the circle.

There was another opening in the circle, and it let in the shrill "Hey Red!", the brief and spasmodic crying of Mrs. Brown's youngest son, the roar and whine and rise and fall of car motors and squeak of brakes and screech of tires and voices, voices moving like birds in the black air around him. Sometimes those voices came closer and became more than voices, swimming to him in the darkness and hitting solid in a handshake so that it was a hand speaking: "Hello there, Arthur"—a calloused hand floating into his circle, or a hard hand would fasten itself on his arm at a street corner, coming in out of nowhere and then the voice would tell him there was something more than the floating hand, a voice saying, "You want to go 'crost now, Arthur? Come on, let me hep you 'crost before that boogering light changes or some of these here fools run you down."

His own hands were like separate things from him, like little animals loose and apart from the black circle, but nevertheless somehow a part of him. It was as though he were one place and his hands—the feeling animals—were loose outside, but somehow he always knew what they were doing. Sometimes they seemed very large, larger than he was, larger than the circle. They would pounce upon things—settling their five little "legs" on another person's hand, capturing a strange thing in the night and pulling it into Arthur's circle so he would know he was not alone, not just a floating black spirit. They would grasp the guitar and dance on the strings—his thumb and forefinger rolled on the strings and the fingers of his other hand bit into the strings so that the hands welded into something else and thus tied Arthur to something else. The music from his guitar was another thing that he could bring into the circle to keep him from being alone inside.

"Hey Red!"

This shout was like a person to Arthur. He didn't know the color red or any other color; he didn't think in terms of color. Red was just an object—a familiar object like the music from his guitar, and it had nothing to do with a fat boy in overalls. It was a thing that existed somewhere and came into the circle to excite his imagination, to stir his curiosity. Sometimes Arthur would grasp his head and feel it, trying to define its boundaries, the hard cage that he could feel, and to understand that all the black circle of himself was held inside and that all the other things that came into it were from somewhere else. It fascinated Arthur to feel of his skull and to know that the black consciousness was held in so small a space.

Suddenly the hickory-switch voice of Shack cut through the blackness: "Stop what y'all doing, People, and come over here. Let the grinding be low, let the plowshare rest in the ground and heed what I say: I've brung a sign from the Lord."

Arthur's fingers felt of the guitar strings, but he didn't play. He listened to the cracking, limber-stout voice of Shack, and he heard a crowd gathering.

Shack held a large ball of rags rolled tightly together as he looked into the faces. "They went and burnt my church over in Scuppernong," he said. "They burnt her down, but they didn't destroy His church, and they didn't destroy His servant Shack. It was a sign. It was a sign from the Lord, and I understand it. It was the Lord speaking, just as he spoke to Moses in a burning bush, and I've come to warn you."

He took a match from his pocket and, raising his leg high to make the pants tight, struck it on the seat of his breeches and set fire to the cloth ball.

"Hey Red! Hey Red!" the fat boy cried, then he sat down again.

Shack held the burning ball high so all but Arthur could see, and more people left the sidewalks to join others on the lawn.

"This is how it's gonna be!" Shack shouted. "This is the way this old world is gonna look one a these days."

"What's he doing?" asked Arthur. "What's he doing?" No one told him. Arthur felt of his head, orienting himself again as to what was inside and what was out.

"They burnt my tabernacle down," Shack said, "but that was just a building, and the Lord showed me where I been wrong. I been thinking about a building. I been preaching in a house. I just been preaching on Thursdays because I'm a Thurs-Day Adventist, but from now on I aim to preach wherever and whenever He wants me to preach, and y'all better listen to me, People."

The ball was blazing, but Shack continued balancing it on the fingertips of one hand.

"It's gonna burn him," someone said.

"What is?" asked Arthur.

"This is the way it'll be," said Shack. "This is the way it'll be in the final day when the trump shall sound, and time won't be no more. Oh no, don't worry about me getting burned. I could hold this ball of rags until it turns to ashes, and it wouldn't hurt me none. It ain't nothing like what's going to happen, and it won't be no long time off, neither. This old world is going to burn. The end of time is nearly here, and all the wickedness and sin is going to be wiped away, and all of you who are not ready are going to be cast into the everlasting lake."

"Where is the lake, Mama?" asked Mrs. Brown's oldest son.

"Shhh. You listen now," Mrs. Brown said. "This is like Sunday school." She sat with her back toward Shack, looking out in the street, watching the people go by, craning their necks to see what was going on. Some of the cars stopped and double parked. From time to time, Mrs. Brown looked around at the ball of fire.

Finally, after flames had scorched his shirt sleeves and licked away hairs on his hand and blackened his fingers, Shack tossed the burning rags onto the grass. The brown and white dog, until then dozing, jumped with a yelp and ran to one side. He came back and barked at the fire, ran to it, backed off, and then Flank Busby, who had come to stand behind the bush where the dog had lain, shooed the animal away.

Shack preached hard, moving on the sidewalk, crouching, dropping to his knees in the grass, warning, imploring, shouting.

"You are a worldly people! You—you back there young lady with them sinful clothes on," he yelled, pointing to a young girl in red shorts. "You orta be ashamed."

Arthur wondered what the sinful clothes looked like. He wondered what a young lady looked like.

"Oh, you've showed your nakedness. You women have paraded it without shame . . ."

Mrs. Brown spoke aloud. "He's right," she said, eying the shorts-clad girl." I wouldn't wear no get-up like that at home, let alone on the streets."

"What? What'd you say, Mama?"

"Nothing," she said. "Shhhh." She looked across the street, still mumbling: "Show their little butts off and don't know from Adam. Probably squeal like a stuck hog. Like I told Prock and them. Better leave them tender little pullets with their hind-ends sticking out alone if they don't want to land in jail. Shack's right. She orta be 'shamed."

"You've painted your lips and cheeks and showed your naked bodies, but the day of nakedness will soon be over. It's not just the women, either. You men, too, running around here with your shirts peeled off. But the days of nakedness will play out when the trumpet sounds."

Mrs. Brown saw Flank Busby slinking behind the bush. She wondered why he hadn't ever been to see her, back from the Navy and all. She wondered if he was anything like his daddy Joe.

"And your filthy books will burn, too," Shack said. "Oh, I've seen them! Seen them in the drug stores and on the counters. I've seen them lusting-sheets put out there for all to see—y'all are a sinful people, and the day of reckoning is near. Thank you can go out here and sow seeds of nakedness and lust and get by with it, but the harvest is coming. It's coming! It's coming, and it's coming right here in Whitt City and in Scuppernong and . . ." His voice caught on the word Scuppernong, and he returned to it:

"Yes Scuppernong. Scuppernong. Woe unto Scuppernong!"

He almost whispered it. "The Lord's judgment shall be upon Scuppernong, mark what I say.

"In the evening when the voices are low, vengeance will come to Scuppernong. But a greater vengeance will come to the whole world. Yes, it's a-coming, People, and the world what you love so sweetly will be destroyed like rags a-burning."

The people watched and listened. Most of them knew Shack, but they had never seen him like this. Even those who had heard him preach in the old schoolhouse recognized a new zeal. He was louder and somehow stronger. And sadder. They moved closer as he continued to tell of the last days in which he said they were living. He told of Noah. He told of wars and rumors of wars. He told of earthquakes in divers places, and he named their sins one by one.

Flank, peering through the limbs of the bush, could see Shack's back. He also could see Mrs. Brown, but he stopped looking at her because seeing her made him think of other women in other places. He thought of Japanese women on straw mats and of the sweet hair oil they wore, and he was ashamed. He must be careful with Margaret. He must be careful so that nothing ugly ever came about between him and the girl with the angel face. He listened closely.

Flank felt guilty about being in the schoolhouse with Margaret and about the fire, which had started from *his* cigarette. But there was more than guilt. He watched Shack, saw his thick hair move as Shack bobbed and weaved on the sidewalk and pounced onto the grass toward his listeners. Shack was a good man, a clean, pure man. Watching, Flank felt a peculiar closeness to the strange preacher. He listened as Shack talked of the end of time. It reminded him of things Sister Busby had said when he was a child, only it didn't scare him so much now as it had then. Somehow, it made him feel better because he had been feeling again that he would die and if everybody else was going, too, then it didn't seem so bad anymore.

Flank watched Shack and felt drawn to him, this strange man who knew so much about everything. This strong, pure man. Flank wished he was clean and pure again; wished he was good like Shack. He wanted to go talk with Shack, to tell him he would help him in the work he had to do, but when Shack had finished talking and when he had prayed, and the crowd was going away, Flank stayed behind the bush, watching, and then Carlton Logan cut across the lawn and stood with his hand on Shack's arm, wanting to talk to him, and Flank drifted back onto the street.

Logan led Shack near the courthouse steps. "You got to help me, Brother Shack," he said. "It's been on my mind ever since that day over at the witching."

"How's Norm's well?"

"Plenty of water. Just plenty. Good water, too, and just exactly where you told him he'd find it. That's what I mean. You got to help me now."

"So he's got good water?"

"Cold as spring water," said Logan. "Just like you told him, and you know what you told me. Said there was a secret in me. Well, you was right, Brother Shack. You was right as you could be, and I'll tell you what the secret is."

"It's money," Shack said. "It's money you're wanting, Carlton. Evil money."

"That treasure's over there someplace," Logan said.

"Sure it's there," Shack said. "The whole bank robbery treasure is there."

"But where?" asked Logan. "I've been searching for years and can't find it. The way you found that water, the way you tell folks things, we can find it, Brother Shack." He was whispering. "If you'd just bring that there witcher-thing over to my place, me and you'd find the money. And I'll split it with you. It's on my place, but I'll give you half of whatever we find if you'll just help me."

"No sir."

"I'll give you whatever you ask then. You could buy that place you been wanting."

Shack looked away. "I wouldn't take a dime of it," he said. "It's evil money. It's got the blood of three men on it."

"Two men," Logan said. "Two men. There were two killed that day . . ."

"Three men's blood," Shack said. "I ain't touching a cent of it. It's wicked money, Logan."

Logan was silent. Shack was the one man he had trusted enough to ask as a partner, and he wouldn't do it.

"Could you loan me your witcher, then? I can find it if you'd just loan me your witcher."

"You don't need no witcher," Shack said. He took a long breath. "You hear my message while ago?"

Logan nodded. "Part of it, Brother Shack, yessir. I hate I missed a word of it. It was inspiring to hear. It was truly a blessing."

"You heard me say the end of time is near?"

"Yessir, I heard that part."

"Heard me say the world's going to burn up?"

"That's why I want to find it," said Logan. "My time's running out, too. I'm getting old, Brother Shack."

"Not too old to lust for money—blood money, wicked money."

"Well, I don't know as how it's going to harm nobody."

Shack looked at him intently, the way he had looked at him on that other day. "You're going to find it," he said. "You're bound and determined to find it, Carlton Logan, in spite of what I tell you. So go on and find it. But you'll see the day when you wish you'd never heard of no buried treasure."

"I don't know where to look no more," Logan said. "I've looked everywhere. Can't you help me, Brother?"

Shack was silent. He looked over Logan's head, then he gazed at him. "You've searched and dug all over the ground, and yet it ain't ever been found," Shack said. "But Carlton Logan, before you die, you'll find what you seek, way up high."

Logan studied a minute. He was disappointed.

"That you said up yonder about an 'everlasting grin in a high place,' I know what that meant. I don't know how in God's name you knowed, but I know exactly what you meant."

"Well," Shack said, and he started to walk away.

Logan caught his sleeve. He had to talk about it.

"How'd you know what I had in my barn loft?" he asked. "Nobody under the sun knowed about that except me, I thought, but you knowed it. I know that's what you meant. I went home and looked, and when I seen them teeth in that skull, I knowed what you meant by 'everlasting grin.' Brother Shack, I didn't do it. I didn't kill that man. I found them bones, found that skull, swear I did, and hid 'em in my barn."

"I know it," Shack said.

Logan shook his head. "I don't know how you knowed. I never told nobody. That's why I know you can help me find it, Brother Shack. I don't see why you won't help me. You could tell me exactly where it is."

"I have," Shack said. He walked off down the sidewalk.

"That's the dadblamest thing I ever seen," Logan said aloud.

"Want a shopping bag, Mister?" Arthur asked.

"Hey Red!" the fat boy with overalls cried.

Mrs. Brown started walking toward the cafes with her two boys. The brown and white dog returned to his shade under the bush.

Chapter 10

It was a young summer night. Tiny green bugs stuck to the screen door of Shack's front door, and it was cool and sweet smelling the way it is before nights get hot and humid in Alabama. Shack was alone at the kitchen table. A glass of milk sat in his plate with chunks of cornbread crumbled in it. Shack was dipping the bread out with a spoon. A bowl of black-eye peas sat on the table. Pearl and Margaret had removed everything else, and Pearl was washing dishes while Margaret dried them with a cloth.

Peeter had caught a large green moth with brown circles on its wings, and he was in another room, adding it to his collection. He had stuck a pin through the small head until the moth stopped fluttering. Now he placed it in a cigar box on a layer of cotton.

"Don't seem like it," Shack said.

"Like what?" asked Pearl.

"I said it don't seem like it."

"What don't?"

"What I'm thinking about."

"Oh."

He took another spoon of bread from the glass. "Been nine years tomorrow," he said.

Pearl kept the dishes quiet, her hands in the soapy water, waiting for him to continue.

"Nine years tomorrow night," said Shack.

Now she knew. Her hands moved with the dishes again.

Shack turned to face her. "It was all over me," he said. "His blood. All over my face and my shirt and everywhere. I felt *his blood* in my eyes."

Pearl remembered the night.

"I seen him drop right in two in front of me. He just broke in half. I mean I seen him, Pearl. And blood splattered all over me and me holding on by just my fangers and wondering how long I was going to be able to hold on and that old train rumbling just a rumbling and a shaking and a tremblin' all over, and me with blood streaming all down my face, and it felt like my fangers was going to slip off of there, and I didn't think that train would ever get acrost, and Hoyt he looked at me. Just once, he looked right at me, and I could see him plain as day with the moon shining, and his eyes just kinda rolled over like they was going to pop out, and he said something. I know nearly-bout he said 'Shack' and then his blood was all over me, and I seen him roll off the side of the track just from here up of him rolled off the side of the track and across them crossties sticking out there and kept rolling and went right off, and I seen it drop into the water down there, and I heard it splash, and I thought just at first even though it was his blood all over my face, I thought well, old Hoyt got out of it after all.

"I thought old Hoyt done rolled loose and ain't hurt or nothing, and then I seen the rest of him laying inside the tracks because the train was done gone, and his britches was laying there, and it had just sliced across his stomach and his legs was laying there just like anybody's legs, and I could feel his blood dripping down my face."

Shack had come to the door past midnight, and Pearl was awake; she never was asleep, and she went to the door because he was banging on it, and the screen was latched so she went to the door and opened it, and Shack was standing there with blood all over, and she thought he was drunk. She smelled liquor, but then she saw he wasn't drunk, and his face, under the blood, was all drawn, and his eyes were hollow, and he was talking in a loud whisper, and she thought he was hurt, and she thought some husband had shot him, and he kept saying, "Hoyt's in Hell. Hoyt's gone to Hell."

And Shack never came home drunk again. And he never went to see any of his women again. And from that night on, the man she had married and known all those years and loved was gone.

"I coulda saved him," Shack said now. "All I had to do was grab hold and pull him over there with me, and Hoyt wouldn't be in Hell tonight."

"You couldn't hope him, I don't reckon," Pearl said.

"I coulda just grabbed ahold and pulled him off of that track. It sliced him right across the stomach and me just hanging there, and I forgot all about Hoyt until I seen him roll out from under that train. I coulda done something, and Hoyt wouldn't be in Hell tonight."

"You couldn't be a-thinking about Hoyt with the train coming."

"I couldn't be a-thinking because I was drunk as a dog," Shack said. "Me and him was both drunk, and if I hadn't got hold of that crosstie, I'd be in Hell with him. And I was the one that got him drunk. He wouldn't of been drunk that night if I hadn't said, 'Hoyt, come on and let's get us a little drink.' I was the one that said it, and I didn't do nothing to get him out from under that train, and the next thing I knowed his blood was running down my face and . . ."

"Somebody's at the door," Margaret said.

" . . . I just hung there and . . ."

"Somebody's at the door, Murphy," said Pearl.

"Huh? Who is it? See who it is, Son."

"He's in yonder. Go see who it is, Daughter."

Margaret started toward the door.

"It's just me," Flank Busby said, looking through the screen.

"Is he drunk?" whispered Pearl.

Flank opened the door and came in before Margaret got there. "Hi, Margaret," he said. "Hello there, Shack."

Shack glared at him. "What's the trouble?" he asked.

"Nothing," Flank said. "Ain't nothing the matter. Go on and eat." He took a chair at the table. Shack smelled liquor.

"What you after?"

"After dark, I guess." He snickered. "Nah, I just come see you. Go ahead on and eat."

Shack turned his glass up and drained it.

"How you getting along, Shack?"

"I'm dog-tired. Been plowing all day. You in trouble?"

Flank snickered. "No more'n usual," he said. "That's my middle name, you know."

"Go on back in there with them dishes," Shack told Margaret. He stared at Flank. Then he put the empty glass to his lips again. "How's Joe?" he asked.

"Joe who?"

"Your papa Joe."

"I don't know. All right, I guess. Was, last time I seen him."

Margaret came to take the bowl of peas away. Flank eyed her.

"You want something to eat?" Shack asked.

"Nah. I about quit eating."

"You drunk?"

"Nah, Shack, I ain't drunk. I just come by to see y'all." He touched his empty shirt pocket for a cigarette, which he already knew he didn't have. "I heard you over at Whitt City the other day. I thought sure you's going to burn your fangers. You done real good, Shack."

"Where you going?" asked Shack.

Flank snickered. "Here, I reckon." He was looking at Margaret. "Nah, I just stopped by to see y'all." He pulled a dirty rag from his pocket and blew his nose.

"Shack," he said, "how come you don't never let that girl go nowhere with nobody?"

Shack glared at him.

"You ought to let that girl go with somebody," Flank said.

"She don't want to go with nobody."

Flank laughed. "Shoot," he said. "Know better'n that. Shoot."

Shack's face tightened.

"She wants to go with me," Flank said. "You just ask her if she don't want to go with me. Tell him, Margaret. Tell him how you been yearning to. You ought to let her, Shack. She wants to . . ."

Shack jumped up, yanked Flank from his chair and threw him to the floor. He piled on and began choking him.

"Mama! Make him stop!"

Pearl clutched Margaret's skirt, but she jerked free, grabbed a broom and ran to where the men were struggling. She swung, hitting Shack's shoulder. She swung again, striking his head.

Shack sprang from the floor and slapped Margaret hard. She stumbled backwards and fell.

"Don't hurt her, Murphy," Pearl said. Peeter was standing in the shadows.

Shack stood over Margaret with his fists doubled. Flank crawled toward the screen door, got up and ran outside.

Margaret was crying. She had her hands over her face. She spread her fingers and looked at her father. "Don't hit me no more, Papa," she whimpered.

"I let one man go to Hell," Shack said. "I let Hoyt go to Hell. I ain't going to stand here and let my little girl go, too."

Slowly he turned and went to the screen door and looked through the paste of green bugs into the darkness.

"Been nine years tomorrow night," he said softly.

Chapter 11

On the night that Shack attacked him, Flank Busby decided to get drunk and stay drunk. Let the devil take Shack and Margaret and Joe Busby and everybody else, and he went to work in earnest toward reaching his goal. He got drunk that night and stayed drunk for a week, and he hardly ate anything except once when he slipped into his father's house and stole money so he could buy more whisky.

By Sunday afternoon he was sober, but he intended to remedy that; he craved a drink in the worst way. So he started walking to Aunt Tessie's house. He had stretched his credit too thin with her, but she was his only hope. Maybe he could tell her he was quitting and needed to taper off. Or maybe he could get her talking about Henry and soften her up. He didn't want to, but if all else failed, he would talk about Sister Busby and tell Aunt Tessie how badly he missed her. Whatever it took, he would do it because he was going to get drunk again—good and wallowing drunk and stay that way. Because now he knew that Flank Busby wasn't worth a damn, never had been, and never would be. It was the only thing to do when you weren't worth shooting.

Great white clouds lay against the blue sky, and they seemed very close to the road. It was hot and dry and farmers needed rain, but Flank didn't care if it never rained. He didn't care if the corn burned up in the fields.

Farmers all worried about whether it would rain; they talked about it and whined about it, and it always rained sooner or later, and they always made their crops, and it was always winter again, and then time to plant again, and what a hell of a lot of difference it all made. They lived, they worked the hot fields and pulled sacks through cotton rows in the fall, and they waited for something to happen, they looked for something in it, and there never was anything in it, and you never did change, you never got away from the sorry, worthless center that was yourself.

But a little snort of juice could sure take you away from it, and if he could get enough of it now, he would never come back.

An airplane droned overhead, hidden somewhere in the white hollow of clouds. Jaybirds screeched from trees beside the road, and a dove called from a far-off pasture. Flank saw the rusty tin roof of Aunt Tessie's house. Honeysuckle vines grew around the yard, and gladiolus leaves, half-smothered in Bermuda grass and weeds, stuck out like green blades beside the road. The old bottles, tied to limbs of a sapling in back, moved slowly with a slight breeze. Flank started to hop across the flowers when suddenly he saw a movement in one part of the yard. He stopped. His head swirled. He was sure, though, of what he had seen.

Standing to the right of the house, as real as he had ever been, was Aunt Tessie's late husband Henry, looking straight toward Flank.

Flank felt his stomach go away, felt it drop right through his bowels and disappear. But it *was* Henry, standing near the black wash pot, which was full of petunias. He wore a white shirt with garters around the sleeves and wide green suspenders like he wore when Flank was a boy. Then he wasn't looking at Flank, but at the ground, walking, moving slowly the way Flank had seen him move long ago, moving in the yard, looking for something.

"Hey!" Flank called, once he could say anything. "Hey!"

Henry didn't pay any attention; he just kept walking. Now his back was turned—his tall, stooped back—and he was slowly moving away.

"Hey! Mr. Henry! Wait!" called Flank. "Wait a minute here!"

But Henry wouldn't wait. He wouldn't pay any attention to Flank. He just kept walking. He was about to go out of sight behind the house. Flank called again and then, when Henry still ignored him, and he was afraid the old man would disappear, Flank ran across the yard, crying, "Wait, Mr. Henry!"

The old man looked over his shoulder once, then broke into a run. It was the first time Flank had ever seen him run. Flank ran faster, afraid of what would happen if he caught the old man, yet afraid he would not catch him. He chased Henry around the end of the house. The old man turned the corner and cut back behind the house. When Flank got to the corner, Henry was gone.

Flank called loudly, but Henry was nowhere. The grass and weeds, knee deep back there, were not bent or in any way disturbed. Flank shook like a wet dog. He jumped wildly when Aunt Tessie, standing near the front porch, spoke to him. "What is it, Boy?"

Trembling, Flank bolted to her side. "I seen him!" he cried. "I seen Mr. Henry."

"Well," she said.

"I mean your husband, Aunt Tessie. I mean your dead husband. He was standing right here. He was walking around right here in this yard. Come right around this here house. I seen him!"

Aunt Tessie chuckled. "Yes," she said. "Henry likes the yard."

"I hollered at him. I hollered to stop, but he commenced running, and I couldn't catch him, and he disappeared. I seen him go around the house right there, and then I didn't see him again."

Aunt Tessie crossed her arms on her bosom and spat into the grass. "These petunias need some water," she said. "Drying smack up if it don't rain."

Flank sat on the edge of the porch. "Aunt Tessie, how long's Mr. Henry been dead?"

"Huh? Henry? Oh. Law Boy, it's been twelve years at least since Henry died. Pshaw, yes, it's been a long spell."

"But I seen him! He was walking right through your yard."

She chuckled again. "Law, he's always doing that. He comes up here heap a times when I'm here to myself. He comes up on the porch and sets with me sometimes at night when the lights are all out. He don't want no lights."

"People don't come back like that," Flank said. He jumped to his feet and grabbed her arm. "He's dead, he can't come back. He's out there in the graveyard."

Aunt Tessie bent over her petunias. "Just drying up," she said.

"He is dead, ain't he? I know he is. I remember his funeral. I seen the hearse pass by our house. I know he's dead."

She straightened and looked at Flank. "He wore a blue serge suit," she said. "It was Sunday afternoon, and it come up a cloud like it was going to storm while we was in the graveyard."

"You seen him dead, didn't you? You know he's dead, don't you, Aunt Tessie?"

"He looked good in that blue suit," she said. "But it rained something awful before I got back home. Henry remembers it. Me and him talk about it sometimes."

Flank wasn't sure now whether Aunt Tessie was alive. He wasn't sure whether the house was really there. His stomach was back, quivering like a big bird somewhere in his bowels.

"You sick, Boy? You want some medicine?"

Flank shook his head.

"I'll let you have some. You don't have to pay me now."

"No'm, thank you."

Flank walked through the yard. When he was almost to the road, he looked back. Aunt Tessie was bent over the wash pot, poking a finger in the dirt around the petunias.

Flank started running. He ran all the way to Shack's house, and his pants was wet when he got there. Shack was sitting under a Chinaberry tree, reading his Bible. Flank fell on the ground beside him. He was out of breath and could not talk. Fear had tightened its grip on him so that it was impossible for him to say anything until after Shack had grabbed his shoulder tightly.

"Is it the Spirit?" Shack asked. "Or are you drunk again?"

"No," Flank said. "No, I ain't drunk, Brother Shack," he gasped. "I just seen a ghost."

Shack watched closely.

"I just seen Mr. Henry."

"Henry's been dead ten years."

"Twelve! But I seen him. Seen him walking in his yard."

"Maybe it was somebody else."

"I know Mr. Henry. I know him well's I know you, and it was him plain as day, and he run from me. I chased him, and he run off from me. I know it was him."

Margaret came to the porch and sat in the swing, but Flank didn't pay any attention to her. He told Shack everything that had happened, all that he had seen.

"It's a sign," Shack said.

"I seen him plain," Flank said. "He was real. Real as you."

"It's a sign from the Lord," Shack said. He seemed very pleased. "I thought the Lord was dealing with you. He has put His hand on you."

"What must I do?"

"Serve Him. Be His vessel."

"How? Tell me what I got to do."

"Yep," Shack said, and smiled. "It's the Lord." He looked toward the house and smiled again. "The Lord wants you, Son."

"I'll do whatever on Earth He wants," said Flank. He got on his knees and clutched Shack's arm. "Let me help you," he begged. "Let me help you, Brother Shack."

Shack looked deep into Flank's eyes. "You not just scared, are you?"

"No sir." Tears were in Flank's eyes. He felt better than he had ever felt. He wanted to hug Shack. He gripped the arm tightly.

Shack covered Flank's hand with his own. "The Lord's demanding," he said. "He's a jealous God, Son."

"I want to serve Him."

"Yes. Yes, I believe you do." Shack looked toward the house again. Margaret was still sitting in the swing.

"You gotta give up things," Shack said. "If a man's going to serve God, he's got to give up father and mother."

"I don't care," Flank said.

"And he's got to deny the flesh."

"Yessir."

"He's got to modify the flesh."

"Yessir."

"You willing? You willing to give up everything?"

"Yes sir. What can I do? You tell me what I got to do."

"We'll see. We'll see what it is He wants of you. But first, you gotta be sure you going to give it all up. Ever thing."

"You just tell me," Flank said.

"You been making eyes at my little girl."

"I won't be doing that no more."

"It ain't pleasing to the Lord."

"No sir."

"You gotta give her up. You got to modify the flesh. Listen. I give it all up. I modified the flesh. You got to forget about Margaret. You hear? You got to give all that up."

Flank sat on the ground listening. He felt very warm and close to Shack. After awhile, Shack quit talking and they sat quietly. It was cooler now.

"He was just walking in the yard like he use to. Just walking in his yard and looking down at the ground."

"It was a sign," Shack said. "It was the Lord speaking to you." He looked toward the house again and smiled. "It's an ainser to prayer," he whispered.

#

Chapter 12

To Flank Busby, it was the happiest, sweetest time of his life. Juicy cornstalks were growing. It rained, not enough, but enough to keep the crops from dying, and green blades waved in the fields. Peas and beans and garden things were green and bearing, and watermelons were getting ripe.

In the mornings, before sunshine dried the dew, Flank would stop in a tomato patch and select one or two of the big red juicy tomatoes, wipe the dust and moisture off, and eat the delicious tomatoes. He stopped at whatever patch was closest because he felt now that it was all right, that nobody minded because he was a part of it all. He had even worked some since his experience with Mr. Henry's ghost, plowing here and there or hoeing a garden where help was needed.

Flank took his meals from the fields, pulling a roasting ear from a young cornstalk and eating the soft green kernels raw or sometimes he would bake them over a roadside fire, and sometimes he ate with Scuppernong farm families. Any time he was asked, he accepted because he felt that he was welcome, and also it gave him a chance to talk with the people, and this is what he most wanted. Sometimes he stayed with a family for two or three days, doing odds and ends around the house, patching fences, working in the gardens, doing anything they wanted done and helping in any way he could. If they paid him, it was all right, and if they didn't, it was all right; the main thing with Flank was to help someone.

He moved into an abandoned shack on the back side of Sim Crawford's farm, but he spent as many nights away as he did at home. Often he slept under the stars. He let his beard grow, and his hair was long.

Flank spent long hours consulting with Shack. He joined him in the fields and around the barn, and they talked while Shack worked. Flank went with Shack to castrate hogs and yearlings and to repair hernias in hogs and to doctor sick animals. He was happiest when he was close to Shack. Sometimes he went to Shack's house and ate supper with him, and after supper they moved to the porch and sat in the cool of the evening, talking far into the night. When Flank was there, Shack made Margaret go to another part of the house. She didn't want to go, but he ordered her.

One night, though, Shack's stomach was cramping, and he went to the kitchen to look for some baking soda, and while he was inside, Margaret slipped out the back door and around to the front porch. Flank was in the swing, and she sat with him. She was bolder than she had ever been—there was a bit of desperation in her voice and in her movements. She clutched at his hand, but Flank put his hands in his pockets.

"I got to talk to you," she said.

"I can't," said Flank. "I can't talk to you. I'm working for the Lord now."

"The Lord don't care if you talk to me. Look at me! Look at me, Sweetheart," she begged. "Just look at me again. Like you done up there in the church."

"Brother Shack explained it to me," Flank said. "It ain't pleasing."

"It's mighty pleasing!" Margaret said. "Don't listen to Papa. Please, Sugar! Like you done up at the church."

"I ain't going to," Flank said. "Get on away now."

"You kissed me," she said. "It wouldn't hurt you none to do it again. You done it onc't, up there. Done it more than onc't. It wouldn't hurt you none."

"I ain't never going to again," Flank said. "I know I done it up there, and I feel bad about that, and the Lord punished us for doing it because He burned down the church house, and it's a plumb wonder me and you didn't get burned up, but He spared us. He give us one more chance, and I ain't never going to act like that again."

"I wish you'd do it again. It felt good to me even if it didn't to you."

"I ain't never going to. You go on now. Brother Shack explained to me about it. He said you'd tempt me. But I ain't going to do it. I told him what we done. I told him everything that ever happened, and he knows I ain't going do it again. He forgave me, and he told me you'd be a-tempting me. Get on, now."

"I guess it's because I'm so ugly."

"Brother Shack explained to me that I got to modify the flesh . . ."

"Well, modify it with me, Sweetheart!"

"Nosiree. I'm working for the Lord now."

Margaret was crying. "I ain't never felt like that before," she said. "You don't care how nobody feels, and I reckon it didn't make you feel like it done me. But you *could* look at me. Can't you even look at me?"

Flank looked straight ahead. He kept the swing moving. Crickets called from the edge of the porch, and the chain of the swing creaked.

"I knowed you wouldn't," Margaret said. "I been waiting for my chance to talk to you, and I hoped you'd look at me again and kiss me again. Ain't nobody else never done it, but I knowed you wouldn't. Only I hoped . . . I sure had hoped so. But I knowed better. Ain't nobody in the world ever going to kiss me again. Ain't nobody wants to even look at no ugly girl like me."

She planted her feet on the floor and stopped the swing's movements. She wiped her nose on her arm. Then she got out of the swing and slunk off the porch and into the yard. Flank heard her crying as she went around toward the back.

Flank had found various ways to be of service. On Saturdays he went into Whitt City on what he considered very special missions. He carried with him a small pair of scissors and went to the book racks in the drug store. Carefully, hiding behind the wire racks that were laden with paperbacks, many of them with pictures of seductive-looking women on their covers, he did his work. Selecting various books and pretending to read them, he looked for naughty words, and when he found them, he would slip his little scissors from his pocket and snip the pages, or snip the evil portions from the pages. Later, because it got to be a problem to dispose of the clipped pages and also because the shrunken books were apt to attract attention, he changed tactics.

There was another reason why he gave up the scissors, too. One day when he went into Wilder's Drug Store and slipped to the back corner, he was accosted by the owner, Claude Wilder.

Mr. Wilder saw him when he entered and left the prescription counter and walked quickly to the rear of the store. He was old and wore thick glasses. His head was entirely bald, and he had a pug nose. The huge horn-rimmed glasses looked much too large for the naked little head, and the nose seemed inadequate to support them. He squinted at Flank and leaned his head toward him.

"Here, what the hell are you up to?" he asked. His face was crimson.

Flank snickered. "Wye, I'm just looking at these here books."

"You ain't neither!" Mr. Wilder spat his words out, struggling to keep his voice low so as not to attract attention of customers elsewhere in his store.

"I know what you're doing. I oughta kill you, Mister. I ought to just throw you down right here and stomp the living hell outta you. How come you cutting up my books? Huh? I saw what you did last week." He gouged his finger in Flank's stomach. "You mangy little long-haired, skinny-legged, shaggy-chinned, simple-minded idiot! I'm going to throw you under the jail."

"Wye, I just . . ."

"You just stood back here and whacked up my books! Who do you think you are to come in here and whack up my books?" He was crowding Flank; Flank had backed as far as he could. A stack of magazines stuck in his back. Mr. Wilder gathered a handful of Flank's shirt and pushed his knotted fist into Flank's stomach.

"They sinful!" shouted Flank.

"Hush! Hush!" Mr. Wilder said through clenched teeth.

"Them's sinful books, that's how come I cut them. You oughta be ashamed selling filthy books like that."

Customers clustered around, watching, giggling. Some nodded and said, "The boy's right, Claude." Others speculated as to what Claude Wilder might do.

"Watch the old man. Watch him now! He's liable to poke him."

"If he don't have a stroke first!"

Flank kept shouting accusations, and the old man, frustrated and embarrassed at the crowd, got louder, too, and kept jabbing

Flank's stomach. In a little while, a policeman came in and at Mr. Wilder's request arrested Flank.

Flank couldn't have cared less. It gave him an opportunity to tell the officer and the jailer, and later the judge, what he thought about dirty words in dirty books. He was charged with destroying private property. Shack made his bail and paid his fine.

After that, Flank was more subtle. He didn't go back to that drug store, but he went to other places that sold the objectionable books. Only he didn't use scissors anymore. He carried a little rubber-tipped bottle of glue, and when he found pages that he didn't think should be exposed to the public eye, he simply glued the edges of the pages together. He even went to the public library and touched up some of the books there. The librarian, seeing his beard and dirty clothes, thought he was a writer, and she treated him very nicely.

Shack said it was a good work that Flank was doing, but he suggested that he be more careful. The satanic forces were, he said, a very vengeful group.

#

Chapter 13

The next time Peeter saw Lily up close was in late June. He was sitting in the shade of trees at the edge of a new-ground field where the first-year corn was growing. It was in a pocket of the woods. He and Shack had grubbed out bushes so they could plant corn. He had been plowing around the young sprouts. The mare stood at the end of a row. The leather plow lines were wrapped tightly around the plow handle to hold the animal in tow. Peeter's shirt, wet almost solid, was unbuttoned, and sweat made a little stream down the center of his chest. He ran his fingers down the tiny trickle. Beads of water stood on the young black hairs of his chest.

Peeter watched a horsefly that sat comfortably on the mare's sleek rump. When he got up again, he would smash it with his palm. He wondered if it would be full of horse blood.

He had seen Lily in her yard—she always waved—several times since the day she came to the field, but he had not talked with her. He thought of her every day and said her name many times. When he was alone, he said it aloud, rolling the name on his tongue: *Lil-ly*.

Sometimes when he said it, he thought of a white lily, like the water lilies he had seen a long time ago before Shack had stopped taking him fishing. Late, late, just before dark, they had stood close to the water in the marshlands, fishing for bream, and the lilies, white—very white against the flat dark green pads in the darkening water—had been the last thing to fade away while the mosquitoes hummed and Shack talked.

Sometimes Peeter wrote her name. At home he did when no one was near. Sitting in the house, reading, with others in the same room, he wrote: "Lily. Peeter Loves Lily. Sweet Darling Lily." Then he scratched it out quickly so no one else would see it.

He had written **L I L Y** on the rough boards of the outhouse wall, then marked through it. Now, cooling in the shade, he took a stick and wrote it in the sand, rubbed it out, smoothed the sand, and wrote it again and again. He had wild wonderful dreams about Lily, dreams which ended in strange mysterious and confusing ways that he could remember happily, warmly, in the daylight.

Peeter took a drink of water from a jar and wrote her name again in the sand. He was writing it when he saw her coming, like magic, toward him along the edge of the woods, in the shade of the trees. Quickly he rubbed out the letters.

She was barefoot, and the faded blue dress looked as though it were all she had on. She wasn't wearing a sash, and her round stomach pooched against the dress like a small melon. She stopped in front of Peeter with her legs spread, and her hands on her hips.

"I figured you was over here. You hiding from me?"

"Naw."

"What's in that jug?"

"Water."

"Oh." She laughed. "Thought maybe it was 'shine. You ever drunk any 'shine?"

"No."

"Never even tasted it?"

"Uh-uh."

"I have. One night I swallowed so much it made me drunk as a coot, and I fell off the front porch and liked to have killed myself, and Daddy whupped me besides. He was aiming to sell it."

Lily sat on the ground. One leg made a tent out of the dress so that her other leg, stretched flat, showed far above the knee. She poked her foot toward Peeter and wiggled her toes. "What you looking at, Dummy?"

"Nothing."

"Are, too." She looked at the mare. "That old horse ever had any babies?"

"Not since we had her."

"Can she have 'em?"

"I reckon so."

"Why don't y'all breed her, then?"

"He don't want to."

"You ever seen 'em breed a horse?"

Peeter nodded. He was chewing a leaf.

"Gahhh! You seen 'em? I ain't never. Not a horse. I've seen bulls up doing the old one-two-three dokey-doo-lolly, but a horse? Why don't you get old Shack to breed her?"

Peeter reached and put his hand on her bare foot, his trembling fingers squeezing hard.

"You devil!" She laughed and shoved him. He grabbed her foot again, squeezed it, and raised it so that her leg came high, and the dress fell away.

Lily slapped the hard sand to keep her balance. "Quit!" she said. "That hurts."

Peeter grinned and kept his hand on her foot.

Lily caught his arm and pulled herself to a standing position. She leaned against him and put her fingers in his hair. Peeter didn't look up at her, but her leg brushed his face.

"Let's go down yonder," whispered Lily.

"Down where?" He didn't know if he could stand. Lily held his hand, and he pulled up, and she leaned heavy against him, and put her mouth against his, and he almost fell. He had absolutely no sense now, and he wasn't sure he would ever breathe again. He clasped at her, grabbed for her, but she stepped away, still holding his hand, and led him into the grass bordering the field.

Peeter glanced toward the corn and thought how he ought to tie the horse to a bush but didn't. Instead, he followed Lily as she walked along the edge of the field to a lower place where rain water had cut a swath as it drained into the woods. It was sandy there, and vines grew everywhere and caused a shady place. Lily turned his hand loose and stooped so she could get under the vines. She lay on the sand and looked at him, standing outside.

"Come on," she said, giggling. "It's cool under here."

Peeter felt crazy and weak and bursting and tried not to let her hear his breathing. He saw the brown legs against the sand and Lily's hand slightly, casually, pulling the faded dress slowly like a curtain. Clumsily, he plunged, falling beside her.

"Ain't it cool in here?" Lily said. She pretended to tug at the hem of her dress. "I can't keep this old dress down," she said. "What you looking at, Crazy?"

Peeter didn't say anything.

Lily giggled. "I could really show you something," she said. "I don't guess you'd want to see, though. Nah, you don't. You'd ruther plow."

"Uh-uh," he said weakly.

Lily held the dress in both hands and slowly raised it, higher than it had been, almost too high. "Gahhh!" she said, giggling. "I wisht you could see your face!" She flipped the hem of her dress, then raised her head off the ground.

"Let's see," she said.

"Huh?"

"Let me see."

Everything was very quiet under the vines. Speckles of sunshine peppered the shady spot. Peeter didn't know what to say or do. He was on his knees. Lily slid toward him. "You 'fraid?"

Just words to hide the work of her busy hands. Tickling his stomach. Touching where the sweat had trickled down. Tugging.

"You 'fraid, say?" She was the only thing not quiet in that shady, sun-speckled place. "Let me see!" Giggling. "Lay down, Dummy."

Her tiny hands were moving like moths, fluttering, then her elbow pressed into his stomach, supporting her as she pulled at his belt with her other hand. "Fraidy cat. Hey, what's wrong? Where you going?" She tried to hold him even after she saw that he was scrambling to get up, saying hoarsely: "Let go! He sees us!"

Peeter pulled free and was staring uphill. Then, she, too, saw through the leaves, down past where they had left the horse, down in the woods from the corn, in plain view, Shack, watching, his wild eyes fixed on them as though in a trance.

#

Chapter 14

Peeter never really went to sleep that night. It was only a half-sleep, filled with erotic visions of Lily, restlessness and curiosity from memories of the episode with her, and apprehension over what Shack would do. Strangely, his fear was at a minimum. He felt detached from Shack, and thoughts of him were overpowered by the sharp memory of the brown-skinned Lily.

Shack had said little, standing and staring for what seemed like a very long time. Then, after Peeter had stumbled back into the field and stood beside the mare, Shack had raised his hand, pointing, and told Peeter to go home. As he walked past the shady alcove, he saw Lily, sitting with her chin on her knees, watching, black eyes moving slyly—caught, but unsurrendered.

Peeter had not talked with Shack again. He had been late getting home, and Peeter, through with supper, went to bed early.

Shack also was having a sleepless night. Lying on his back, staring into blackness, he pondered his options. Pearl, aware only that something was wrong, lay quietly across the room, worrying.

"The devil is in him," Shack said finally.

"In who?"

"The devil has gotten to him," Shack said. He would not explain, and Pearl was afraid. "He's a good boy," she whispered.

Much later, after Pearl's breathing became loud and relaxed, Shack decided. He worked out all the details in his mind, then waited. After midnight he slipped from bed and went to the kitchen where he lighted a lantern and walked outside to the barn.

In a little while he returned with a fruit-jar half-full of clear liquid. He set it on the floor and took his bone-handled knife, which he used for castrating hogs and calves, and started sharpening the blade on a small whetstone. For a long time he moved the blade back and forth, stopping from time to time to spit on the stone and to pull the blade across his thumbnail, testing.

Shack stared at the floor. His lips moved as he thought of the fat, clean steers—his good, pure steers, separated and apart. Then he took the jar of chloroform and the knife and crept to Peeter's room.

It was very dark, so Shack went back for the lantern and placed it on a trunk near his son's bed. The light danced in the room. Peeter's face was strange in the soft light. Shack studied the long body under the sheet. He said a silent prayer. Then he unscrewed the top of the jar and rolled his handkerchief and thrust it into the liquid. Slowly, deliberately, he went about his work. When it was finished, and Shack was gathering his things, he heard Pearl outside the room. He rushed to the door, holding the lantern.

Pearl pushed open the door, eyes wide, her face drawn. "What is it?" she whispered hoarsely. Her eyes darted to the boy sleeping in the shadows. "What is it, Murphy?" she asked again, her voice strained and trembling.

She saw his bloody fingers, clutching a darkened handkerchief. "What's that smell?" she asked. "Murphy! Murphy! What have you went and done?" She clutched his arm, but he brushed past her, into the kitchen. She followed and grabbed his undershirt.

"What'd you do? Murphy! Ainser me!"

Slowly he looked in her direction, then at the lantern. He turned the wick down. "If thy eye offend thee," he whispered, "pluck it out." He looked at her, and she saw the color of his eyes changing.

"If thy right hand offend thee," he whispered, "cut it off. If thy eye offend thee . . ."

Pearl ran to Peeter's room, and Shack, standing in the hall looking at the bloody bundle in his hand, heard her crying and talking to the sleeping boy the way she had talked to him when he was only a baby. Very still, Shack listened. Then he went to the back porch. It would soon be daylight. And the upright shall have dominion over them in the morning . . .

When Peeter finally came through the thick and stifling clouds, back into the pain of day, he saw Mama floating beside his bed, eyes red and puffy. He made the mistake of moving.

"Be still, Sugah-Lamb," she said. Her voice was like a velvet bell. "You got fever, Baby." The hand brought a wet cloth across his eyes. But it did not stop the wave of nausea or the stinging pain. Yesterday. Yesterday. But yesterday—Lily—would not focus, and the hot desire of yesterday had flown, and had that caused this nightmare?

"I don't feel good."

"I know it."

"I might have to thow up."

"Be still as you can."

"How long you been here?"

"All night. Ever since . . ."

"What'd I do?"

"You didn't do nothing, Sugah."

"I dreamt Papa . . . Mama, I dreamt that Papa come in and put a rag over my face. I dreamt he was trying to smother me."

He felt of his head. It should have been larger.

"Oh, Mama! I hurt so bad."

"I know, Sweetheart."

"How come me to dream that?"

"Be still."

"Say, Mama? How come?"

"You wasn't dreaming, Shug."

Wide-eyed, Peeter stared at her. He started crying. "You mean . . .?"

"Don't you know, Baby?"

He raised off the pillow. He whispered, "Like the calves, you mean? Oh, no, no, no!" He lay crying for a long time as Pearl kissed his face and tried to comfort him.

"Am I bad?" Peeter finally asked.

"You didn't do nothing. He done it."

"Where's he at?"

"Outside somewheres."

"Is he coming in here?"

"No he ain't!"

"Don't let him come in here."

"He ain't, Sugah."

"How come, Mama?"

"Because he's mean and crazy!" she cried.

"I can't go to school no more." He cried hard. "I can't go nowhere."

It was quiet in the room. Pearl looked at her hands.

"I ain't going to stay here," he said.

"You got to."

"No I ain't. I'll live in the hollow if I have to, but I ain't staying here."

Pearl cradled him in her arms. "I'll take care of you." She stroked his forehead. "I'll take care of my baby."

"Will you go with me, Mama?"

"We can't go nowheres."

"I can."

"No. There ain't nowheres to go."

"He put that rag over my face and mashed it against my nose, and it burnt, and that's all I know. It wasn't a dream, was it?"

"No," she said. "It was him." She leaned closer. "I didn't know, honest. I was sleeping. I wish . . ."

When Shack came back to the house in the evening, Peeter was sleeping. Pearl followed Shack into their bedroom. She went to the closet and started grabbing dresses and piling them on the floor.

"What are you fixing to do?" asked Shack.

"I ain't going to stay in no room with sech as you."

"You don't mean it."

"I said I ain't staying!"

"How come you acting like this?"

Pearl threw a dress to the floor. "How come you went and treated him like that?" Her voice was raw from crying, and tears streaked her face.

"I had to," Shack said. "I had to do it."

"You never no sech thing!"

"I done it for him."

"No sech thing . . ."

"I done what I thought was best. I love that boy, Pearl."

"Treat him like some old cow! How come you done sech a thing?"

"You know what he was headed for. I told you what he was headed for."

"I don't care."

"He was on the path to Hell, Pearl. I had to stop him. I done it because I love him. I had to."

Her voice rose, screeching: "You didn't have no right to treat him like an old cow. How'd you like it if . . ."

"You know where he was headed. I told you."

"It don't make no difference where he was headed. You . . . you headed for enough of it! Yeah, look at you. Look at you. He wouldn't never do no worse'n you if he was to live to a hundert."

"You're right," Shack said."You're telling the truth. Don't I know what I done? Huh? You think I don't know how much I sinned? I wallowed right on the jaws of Hell, but I promised God I'd make it up to Him. I promised Him the boy wouldn't never do like I done."

"He wouldn't never do what you done."

"I seen to it," Shack said. "I had to. I promised God. I done some mighty wicked things against the Lord."

Pearl stared at him. She was crying again. She wiped her nose on the back of her hand.

"I was wickeder than Satan."

"He'd a forgave you," said Pearl. "He'd a forgave you."

"No, my soul was too black. I couldn't get no forgiveness."

"He'd a forgave you anyhow."

"He couldn't. Not like I was."

"God ain't like you!" Pearl said. "You won't let nobody alone. You 'fraid God won't forgive 'em."

Shack did not answer. Pearl had never talked to him like this.

"Like you going and cutting that gol-derned old fanger off."

Shack glanced at the nub.

"Whyn't you hep the boy? Whyn't you hep him so he wouldn't do nothing he wasn't s'posed to, steada treating him like a . . . a pig! Naw. It's like that old fanger. You ain't going trust nobody theirselves. You ain't even going trust yourself. You got to go and chop off something."

"I done what the Lord told me to do."

"Pshaw! I'd hate to lay something like that on the Lord. You thank the Lord's like you. You thank He ain't going to forgive nobody." Her voice got sick again, and she cried: "How come you treat my baby like that? He's just a little boy."

"He was headed straight to Hell."

"It ain't none of your business where he goes! Why didn't you leave him alone?"

"I reckon you don't care if he goes to Hell?"

"I don't care if you do!" Pearl cried.

She picked up her dresses and carried them to Peeter's room. Later she heard Shack praying in the back bedroom.

Four days later Peeter got up before dawn, dressed, and slipped out of the house with a sack of clothes. Dew wet his shoes, and dust from the road stuck to them. He walked to Sam Antone Rose's house and knocked on the door. Sam was cooking breakfast.

"Why what in tarnation you doing up so early?"

"Can I live here?"

"What you talking about?"

"Can I move in with you?"

"What's the matter, Papa run you off?"

"I ain't living there no more. Can I stay here?"

Sam looked at the clothes stuck under Peeter's arm. He stopped smiling and opened the screen door. "You sick or something? You don't look so pretty good. Lay down, and I'll get you some coffee."

"Can I live here? Say?"

"Why, I reckon so. Go on, lay down on that devinet."

Sam took Peeter's clothes to another room. He poured coffee into a thick mug. Peeter sipped a little of the coffee.

"Boy, you sure don't look so pretty good, you know that? You lay right there. I'll bring you some breakfast."

Peeter didn't talk while he ate, and Sam didn't ask any more questions. He was afraid to find out what had happened.

#

Chapter 15

Carlton Logan's house had never been painted. An L-shaped porch with banisters stretched across the front and halfway down one side. Logan was born there, and he and Effie had lived with his parents until they died. His mother died first, in the second year after he and Effie married, of what they called "heart dropsy." She also had a very sharp tongue, and few neighbors visited her in the last years of her life. Although Effie never admitted it, even to herself, and after Mrs. Logan's death talked of how wonderful the old lady was and how close they had been, she was relieved when her mother-in-law died because there was hardly a day while they lived together that she didn't criticize Effie.

Logan's father lived eight years after his wife died, and the last three years he had been totally deaf. He died of pneumonia.

The house sat on a small hill facing Norm Otwell's backyard. A large pasture separated the houses, and no other dwellings were in sight. Logan liked his house, and if he ever found the buried treasure, he had no plans to tear it down and build a new one although this is what Effie constantly begged him to do.

There had been a time when Logan needed money, years when crops failed, and he had to go to the bank for extra time on his notes, but he didn't really need money now. He had all his land in the soil bank except seventy-five acres that he kept in pasture for a few head of cattle, and in another year he could draw his full Social Security benefits. Because of a few good investments and his parsimonious habits through the years, Logan had about all the money he expected to need for the rest of his life, barring the unforeseen.

Logan gave twenty-five dollars a year to the church—ten dollars a whack at Christmas and the rest in dollar bills, quarters, nickels, and dimes. He always gave it no matter what kind of year he had, and he was proud of this. He cared little for clothes, and he had managed to curb Effie's desire for fancy things. So he didn't really need money as he once had, and he didn't have a particular goal for it if he ever found the treasure. Still, he wanted it as much as it is possible for a man to want anything. The older he got, the more determined he became to find the buried gold. It became harder for him to sleep nights, and he would get angry thinking about all the years he had searched in vain.

After one such sleepless night, Logan slipped out of bed before daylight and started dressing, buttoning his shirt from the top. His mind was busy with the woods, dissecting, plotting. He held his overalls low and stepped into them.

"Where is it this morning, Carlton?"

Effie's voice, always louder than necessary, startled and irritated him. He turned toward it. Bits of reddish-black hair stuck out above the sheet, spread on the pillow like ragged feathers. Two wrinkled prunes, which were Effie's eyes, lay between the sheet and the dyed hair. It looked to Logan like a thing, rather than a person, and he didn't answer it.

A fly circled the bed and hummed close to the black squints of Effie's eyes. She sank into the mattress and covered her face quickly with the sheet. "Nasty fly!" she said. "Worry a body to death." She peeped over the sheet.

A mirror that had belonged to Logan's mother hung on the wall, and he picked out Effie's reflection in it. Her hair had been thin for a long time, so that a lot of her head showed through. The more she tried to stave off the gray, the thinner it got.

"You want me to go along and help you carry all that gold back?" she asked. She laughed down in her throat. Logan fastened the galluses of his overalls.

Effie pulled the sheet down and put her hands under her head and blinked. She smiled, gathering her great lips into a cluster around her false teeth. "Honey," she said, "I'll bet that gold's been gone for years. I wouldn't doubt but what them outlaws took it all with 'em . . . if there ever was any outlaws up there."

Her voice, still filling the room, still running from one sentence to another without pause, had shattered Logan's thoughts. Hurriedly, he pulled on his high-topped rough leather shoes.

" . . . spent half as much time doing that or something like that as you have digging around in the woods, we'd all be better off. Lester bought Alice and him a new Ford, you know that?"

Logan grunted, and she kept going. "You ain't seen that, I don't reckon. Alice's telling the world about it. You'd think it was the only car ever made. I just thought to myself, looks like we could get something new ever once in a while. I just said to myself . . ."

Lord, she was old, and that meant that Logan, too, was old. He remembered a long time before when Effie had been pretty with a lot of hair and tight, smooth skin. Logan looked at the old ragged hair, at the dark walls, at the whole cheerless room, and a cold, sick feeling crept over him.

There was so little to show for all his years. You worked and had nothing. You slept with a bald-headed woman, and there were no children. You hunted, and there was no gold. You walked down through the long tunnel of years, and there was nothing at the end of it. No matter what you did, you just got old and flabby, and in a little while you died, and there wasn't even anything left for people to remember about you. Unless they could say, "He found the gold." Angrily, Logan stalked out of the bedroom, away from the old flabby machine that did the thing it had always done so well—ground out words so fast they almost jammed the opening.

A big gopher rat sat on top of a sack of feed and stared impudently at Logan when he opened the barn door. Logan stomped, and the rat moved, slowly, sullenly, and disappeared into a hole. Even rats were unimpressed.

Logan heard a mule grinding corn. He pulled the door tightly behind him and waited until he could see again. He climbed into the loft where some of the winter hay was stored. Logan walked on the hay in sinking, springy steps, to a dark corner where he stopped and listened before digging away the hay until he came to the box with the bones. This he gathered in his arms and carried to a clearing on the loft floor.

Piece by piece he removed the sooty bones and placed them on the planks. He also removed the gun. Then he lifted the skull from the box, holding it very carefully. It always filled him with excitement to inspect the secret bones. Lord, if he could find the gold!

It was very quiet in the loft. Strings of daylight came from tiny holes in the barn, and specks of dust from hay shone in the light. Logan thought of all the years he had looked and wanted. Thinking about it made him angry.

Some teeth were missing from the grinning skull. Logan felt of the smooth bone that had been the forehead and thought of the man . . . what man? Some man who had wanted the money long ago, and he was gone, had been gone for so long, and the money was still there. Somewhere. It made Logan uncomfortable. It wouldn't be many years, couldn't be many, until he would be like the bones that he held in his hand. And the gold, the buried treasure that he had hunted for years, would mean nothing. There was something comforting about the skull, though. It never changed. It looked no older than the day he had found it. Its grin never changed, either. "Everlasting grin," Shack had said. Eternal.

Logan was starting to like the skull better than he liked people, whose hair came out and whose skin sagged and wrinkled. He felt friendly toward the unchanging skull.

Remembering what Shack had said about "high places," Logan spent the morning exploring the hills, but he didn't have much faith in Shack anymore. He didn't appreciate Shack's attitude toward the whole thing. So after awhile, he gave up on the hills and went back for the hundredth time to the place where he had found the bones and started digging. Frantically, he attacked the ground with a shovel until he had turned the earth over a wide area. All he found were bits of glass and a rusted sardine can.

Exhausted, he lay on his back and rested. He dozed and dreamed of former days, of his parents and older brothers, all dead now. When he awoke, he was sad, and he lay still and quiet, looking into the trees.

A great oak was near; its branches shaded Logan. He looked at the gnarled trunk, at the gray stuff on its bark, and at the underside of leaves. The trunk forked high above the ground, and something attracted Logan's attention in the fork. He kept gazing at it, a spot of something that didn't match the bark. He sat up and stared at the spot, then stood and craned his neck. There was a hole of some sort in the crotch of the tree, and the spot—the rusty brown spot—stuck out of the hole. His heart pounded.

It had been many years since Logan had climbed a tree, and it was difficult for him to do so now, but he stuck to it. Several times he slipped back to the ground. Then he pulled his shoes off and finally made it to the limbs and, by the hardest effort, on to the yoke. His hand got there first, and he knew as soon as his fingers dipped into the hollow place that he had found the treasure. He felt old soggy leather!

Quickly, he scrambled the rest of the way and sat astride the great limb. It was a leather bag, molded, mildewed, and rotten. Bird droppings crusted it. With trembling fingers, Logan lifted it from the hollow place, and the weight thrilled him. Holes in the bag had let some coins drop into the rotting center of the tree. Others fell as Logan lifted the bag. Sobs convulsed him.

"By Jacks I found you!" he kept saying. "Old Logan found the gold. Wait'll they hear about Old Logan finding the gold. By Jacks I found it!" He clutched the bag—it was heavy. Lord, was it heavy. Logan mashed the sides, feeling the money lumps inside.

Suddenly, he felt light-headed and weak. It all seemed so very unreal; it was almost too much for him to grasp. He looked below, and this made things worse; everything was whirling and spinning, and he couldn't hold the tree still.

Then Logan fell. He was still holding the bag of gold when he hit the ground.

"Oh, he can't move at all," Effie whispered. "Oh, no, no, the poor thing is completely helpless. Yes, he's paralyzed except for his fingers and toes, and he can move his head just a tee-niny bit. Dr. Crump said it's a thousand wonders he's alive." Tears squeezed out of the two dark prunes.

She stood in the corner of Logan's hospital room talking with Ada Messick and Miz Joyce Crawford. Logan's eyes were closed, and, heavily sedated, he was sleeping.

"There must of been thousands of dollars in that little old sack," Effie said. "Oh, my yes, and solid gold every cent of it. Think of it! I said, Well, it's bad, Logan, and of course I'd rather it hadn't happened than to have all the gold in the world, but I guess we can find a use for it. There's always a bright spot somewhere in everything if we look for it, and of course we'll need ever cent now. My goodness, this room costs us twelve dollars and fifty cents a day, and the Lord knows how long the poor thing will lay there.

"Oh, no, he'll never walk again. No. No." She shook her head to stop Ada's protest. "No, Dr. Crump says he won't, poor thing. Well, I said, money's not ever thing. He hunted so hard for it. I tried to tell him, you know, that money wasn't ever thing, and it didn't matter whether we had any material thing. I'm not used to anything of course, and he talked about a car, and I told him, why Logan, we don't have to have a car. Why, we have no need of a car, I said. But he wanted so much for us to have some- thing. I tried to encourage him and help every way I could, you know. I guess it's my fault, actually, for allowing him to look for that old gold, but he wanted so much to find it, and I tried to encourage him in it because you know that's what I thought a wife was supposed to do, but I shouldn't ever have permitted it, I know that now of course. But I tried to help him in whatever he wanted to do."

Logan had lain on the ground until long after dark before Norm Otwell found him. It took more than an hour for Norm to get help. In Norm's pick-up truck, Logan had talked to the men who sat in back with him. All the way to the hospital, he told them, "Listen to Shack. Do what Shack says. Do you hear me? Listen to that man. Go to him and ask him what you should do, and then listen to him. I wish I had listened."

He had told Norm this first, rather than about the gold. Now on the hospital bed he called Effie.

"Yes Sweetheart? What is it, Sweetheart?"

"I want to see Shack."

"Oh, Honey, you don't need to see Shack now. No, you don't need to see anybody just now. Of course, you can see him later, but not just now . . ."

"I said I want to see Shack."

"Well, now Honey, you just . . ."

"Send somebody for Shack, Effie!"

She looked helplessly at Ada and Miz Joyce.

"Bring Shack to me, Effie," Logan commanded.

"Oh, I don't know, I don't know," she said. "What am I going to do, Ada?"

"I'll get word to him," Ada said. She went to the bed and touched Logan's arm. "I'll get Shack for you," she said. "You don't worry, Carlton, I'll get word to him right away."

Effie followed Ada to the door. "The poor thing's so doctored up," she said. "He don't know. We'll have to humor him, you know."

"Go get Shack," Logan called.

Chapter 16

Late one night Peeter's screams awakened Sam Antone Rose. Sam bounded from his bed next to a window and ran to where Peeter lay on a cot next to the other wall. He shook him until he was awake.

"You having bad night-horses," he said. "Too much catfish for supper. Go on back to sleep."

In a little while, he heard Peeter crying. "What you sniffling about, Bohunkus?"

The room was very dark, and beyond the window was so dark Sam could barely see the limbs of the trees that showed clearly on other nights. It was very still, too. Peeter did not answer.

"You sick at your stomach?"

"Uh-uh."

"Belly hurt?"

"No."

They were quiet again. The house cracked. Peeter and Sam were very quiet for a long time. Then: "Is God crazy or what?"

"Hush, Boy. You trying to get us lightning struck?"

"He hates us when we do bad things, don't He?"

"God likes for folks to sleep at night, that's what God likes."

"What's God look like anyhow, Sam?"

"I don't know!" Sam said. "You think I'm big buddies with God? Huh? You think God takes me cat-fishing in the swamp?"

"You ever done anything real bad, Sam?"

"No, but I'm by cracky fixing to kill me a Bohunk if he don't shut up and go to sleep."

Sam heard Peeter settling down in the bed. He hoped he would stop talking and go to sleep. Sam wasn't used to thinking in the middle of the night. But Peeter spoke again: "If God made every-body, then how come He lets 'em mess up?"

Peeter's words hung in the darkness. Sam didn't answer.

"Say, how come?"

Sam was thinking.

"How come?"

"So He can 'scuse 'em, I reckon."

"Do what?"

"'Scuse 'em! You deaf?"

"Why?"

"Unnnh! Maybe He loves y'all. I don't know. Ask Shack. Go to sleep!"

The trees stood very still in the dark yard outside. Nothing out there moved.

"Papa's worse'n God about not wanting you to do nothing bad. Only he ain't like God. He fixes it so you can't."

"I wish you'd dry up and go to sleep," Sam said.

"He fixed me so's I couldn't ever do nothing bad with a girl. Did you know that?"

Sam held his breath. Then he said, "Your papa loves you, Buddy."

"Then how come he done me like what he does to hogs? How come he ruint me. Huh?"

Sam felt a little sick. He heard Peeter sniffling again. Swearing, he jumped out of bed. "That crazy man done that to you? You not jiving Sam—he done that? Why ain't you told me before?"

"I didn't want nobody to know."

Sam crossed the room and sat on the floor beside Peeter's cot. "You had oughta told Sam," he said. "All this time I coulda been cutting his sorry throat!"

Peeter was sobbing uncontrollably. Sam laid his hand on the boy's cheek. "Damn, damn, damn!" he cried, pounding his other fist against the floor. Then he chuckled. "You little dickens! You had old Sam going there. How come you want to lie to old Sam?"

"I ain't lying," Peeter whispered. "He done it while I was asleep one night. He ruint me. That's how come me to come to live with you."

"I'm sorry, Bohunk. You want me to go kill him, I will. You hear?" When Peeter didn't answer, Sam went to the window

and stood, peering into the darkness. Some time later he heard
Peeter talking quietly; heard him say: "Papa's ain't like God. He
don't excuse nobody."

Sam lay down in his bed. The boy sounded far away.

"He thought he fixed it so he could love me, but he can't."

"Be quiet, now."

"He can't love me on account of I done something bad anyway."

Sam turned on his side and looked toward the window.

"He thought he fixed me so I couldn't, but I done it anyway."

"You ain't done nothing bad your whole life, Boy."

"Yes I did! I found something bad to do anyway." Sam heard him
flouncing. "You know what it is? I just hate his gol-derned old guts."

"Shhh," Sam said. Peeter sounded very excited.

"He'd think that was bad, wouldn't he?"

"Uh-huh. Yeah, that's plenty bad all right."

Peeter kept talking for a long time. But Sam wasn't going to
sleep anymore that night anyway. He felt like squalling himself.

#

Chapter 17

The earth around Scuppernong was like a female. In the spring it came alive like a young girl bursting into womanhood. It was dark and rich and fertile and eager for seed. When the frosts were over, and all threat of snow was past, and the March winds were doing their clean, cool sweeping, and little green sprigs were showing, the farmers split the rich ground with steel blades. They followed their mules in long straight lines, piling a dark fresh border around a plot of hard pale ground until the border closed out the center, and then great quilts of black, turned, soil showed in the fields.

The dried sedge, the rambling briars, the dry cotton and corn-stalks, tiny green sprigs and brittle sticks were covered, and shiny slices of earth lay exposed to the sun. The ground was ready, then, for the seed. It was mellow. It had responded; it was ready to respond further.

Then came the harrowing, with mules pulling the flat, teethed harrow across the fields. Clods burst, and the dirt was leveled and after that the rows were laid off and seed sown. Then the land was like a woman again. It became quiet again. The sun dried it. The rain wet it again, and the sun dried and warmed again, but it was quieter, like a pregnant woman, content and waiting.

After that, the ground became hard again. The corn and cotton came up. Weeds returned, grass grew, but the ground was hard and though it yielded to the plow, though it softened with rain, it was different. It had lost the eagerness and settled into routine; it was no longer receiving, it was giving; the little roots were drawing strength from all parts of it, and it lay listless and lazy like a nursing mother.

Late in July the ground was powder dry and hot. It needed water. In the corn fields, the blades did not look so green; they were coated with dust. The long blades waved their tips lazily when a breeze moved through the rows. The ears were hard and packed inside drying, browning shucks, and the silks, once soft and juicy yellow, were brown and dry and ugly. It was too late to plow.

In the afternoon, Norm Otwell walked down a row in his cornfield. He twisted an ear off a stalk, ripped the shuck open, and pressed his finger against the grains. He pinched off some of the grains and tasted them. Then he hung the ear back on the stalk and walked on. His shoes were dusty, and he wished it would rain.

Norm stopped in his backyard and drew a bucket of water. He held the small round bucket in both hands and drank. It was cool and good. He remembered the day Shack had witched for the well, and he smiled, thinking of what Shack had told him: "Drink it while the sun is warm, Norm, because when the frost is on the ground, it'll be too late."

Well, the sun was warm now, and the water was good. If it didn't rain, there might not be any water by the time of frost, though. That's all Norm worried about, not the "wood and the stone." Norm didn't believe in fortune telling. He didn't really believe in water witching. Shack had been lucky, that was all. Norm thought of his neighbor, Carlton Logan, and of how he had changed since his accident. He could see him on his porch now—could see the figure of Logan and the white sheet that covered him. Logan was still unable to move, but he could talk. Oh, how he could talk.

Norm seldom visited Logan because he didn't like the way Logan talked, filled with warning for everybody, especially for Norm—warnings and pleas for the people to listen to Shack and to heed his advice.

Norm avoided Logan and Shack as much as possible. Strange things happened, that's all you could say. Just that some strange things happened. Well crap, if it would only rain, he would be happy, and if it didn't, his crops wouldn't be worth the effort to take them to the barn. If only it would rain.

Shack even had something to say about that; he was promising rain. A delegation had gone to Shack, asking his help in getting rain. Shack said they would get it, but he had also made a silly prediction that tragedy would accompany the rain. Shack always had to put a little hell fire in everything, Norm thought. This was the only reason he was reluctant for rain to come. If it rained now, they'd all say Shack had brought it. Maybe soon they'd start praying to Shack. Well, there wasn't much chance of rain although there was a small cloud in the west.

Norm's wife and children had gone in to Whitt City. He wished they were home, and he would take Ted to the creek. He felt lonely and somehow closer to Mary Etta and the boys. He was going to start spending more time with them, and there was no need quarreling with Mary Etta as he had done. She was a good woman. Norm lay on the planks of the porch in the sunshine and went to sleep.

In the fields little whirlwinds of dust rolled between the rows. The dusty green blades fluttered as a breeze grew stronger. On the porch, Norm slept, but a cloud had covered the sun. In the barn lot, a mule rolled once, twice, three times, trying to roll over, then gave it up and stood, clumsily, its side coated with dust.

It was still and quiet. White Leghorn hens wallowed in dust. There was hardly any other movement as the afternoon wore on. Dark moving clouds grew larger in the west. Carlton Logan's wife came to the porch and moved him inside. She left a sheet on a chair, and it fluttered in the wind, but Norm did not see it. He was sleeping. Sweat soaked through his shirt and dampened the planks. His mouth was open, and little short snores came from it. In sixty seconds, Norm would be dead.

It came out of the quietness like a freight train, and in his last conscious second this is what Norm thought it was. He heard the roar.

Then Norm and the back porch were swept into the air and carried past the barn. The rest of the house, except the floor, went in another direction. The roof was peeled off Logan's house. Chickens sailed high into the air. The mule that moments before had tried in vain to roll over, was caught in the black swirl and made dozens of complete rolls in the air before being dumped to the ground. Logan's barn was turned around, and Norm's barn was flattened like his house.

Cornstalks in Norm's field were twisted and flattened and ripped up by roots and blown away so that there was hardly one left standing. Great balls of hail pounded the earth, and lightning flashed, and thunder bumped from cloud to cloud.

Then it was quiet again, and only the rain continued, quieter, in smaller drops, and the thunder moved farther away. Weak threads of lightning marked the sky.

It was over in three minutes. Debris littered the yard and pasture. Nothing was as it had been three minutes before. There was hardly a house in Scuppernong that was not damaged. The dead, the injured, were yet to be counted.

Darkness, wet rainy darkness, and quiet fell over Norm Otwell's place and down in the pasture, behind where the barn had stood, Norm lay still, his head smashed between a heavy cedar timber that had been a part of his house, and a big sandstone.

#

Chapter 18

They worked all night retrieving bodies from the wreckage. Clink Stoddard and a group of men from Blue Town brought mules and trucks. Ambulances came from Whitt City, but they had difficulty getting through because trees and debris blocked the roads. Rain continued throughout the night, and vehicles mired in mud. Scuppernong Primitive Baptist Church survived with only a few shingles blown from its roof, and the people quickly converted the church into a rescue center. The hurt and the homeless were taken there. The women rallied as women always do in such times, and by midnight wide-eyed children were bedded down on pallets, hot coffee was there for anyone who would drink it, and the other things that only the women could offer to the shocked and frightened mothers and widows—comfort and understanding—were there, too.

Mary Etta Otwell sat at one end of a pew. A patched quilt covered everything from her neck down. Her blonde hair, which she had set before going to Whitt City, was straight now and hung in separate pieces about her white face. Her eyes were tiny blue hubs for red-rimmed wheels. All lipstick was gone, and her mouth, once full, was a tight little button. Bobby's head was in her lap, and his eyes were open, staring into his mother's face. Ted lay sleeping farther down the pew. Ada Messick came to the pew in front of them and put her hands on the back of it and leaned toward Mary Etta.

"Can you eat something?"

"No, I wouldn't care for nothing right now."

"It's going to be a long night, Sweetheart." Ada reached out and touched the younger woman's hair, then touched her cheek with the back of her hand. "You'll make out," she whispered.

"I wish I'd stayed at home, Miss Ada."

"Well, I don't know if you do. No, Mary Etta, I don't know as I'd say such." She put her fingers under Mary Etta's chin. "When you think about these little boys. When you've had time to think about it awhile, I think you'll be glad the good Lord seen fit to let you be somewhere else. When you think about your little boys."

"I'd like to be with him."

"Of course you would."

The little blue specks sank in tiny pools of water that got deeper until they pushed straight out and plunged down the white face. Ada held a handkerchief to Mary Etta's face. Ada took a deep breath. "Nothing's for certain yet," she said.

"If he could, he'd find us. He ain't there or he'd find us. He ain't there, or he'd already found us by now." She stared at Ada.

"You have to hold up for them boys. You can't . . ."

Mary Etta jerked forward and, pawing a hand from under the quilt, caught Ada's arm. "Do you think Norm's hurt down there someplace?"

Her voice came stronger. "Do you think maybe he's out in all this, hurt someplace?"

"Nothing's for certain . . ."

"Do you?" cried Mary Etta. She started to get up, and Bobby whimpered, but Ada quieted her. "You're just going to have to wait, Honey," Ada whispered. "You've got to hold up for the boys."

On another bench Mae Stout sat with a blanket around her shoulders. Her eyes were like tiny red-clay ditches after a big rain. On each side of her, two women sat. One was a large, fleshy woman. She was smiling.

"Me and this woman been friends a long time," she said to the little dumpy woman on the other side of Mae. "Why, Mae and me have been friends all our lives. Iddn't that right, Mae?"

Mae nodded.

"Why yes, bless your heart, we've been good friends for a long, long time. Yessiree. Why, I don't have a better friend in this world than Mae Stout. That's right, iddn't it, Mae?"

Mae nodded again.

"Yessir. I don't have a better friend in this old world. We've been friends a long old time."

"I felt like something was going to happen," Mae said. "I don't know what I'm going to do."

"A person couldn't want for no better friend . . ."

"He was one of the . . . even if he was my husband, he was a good man. I don't just say it because he was mine, but he *was* a good man. He worked hard all his life." She looked at the dumpy little woman. "He really was a good man," she said.

"Old Mae and me have been friends for many a year," the other woman said.

Eleven people died in the storm. They didn't find some of them until daylight, but when they were all accounted for, eleven were dead. Norm was the last found. His bird dog led them to him.

Dead were:

Norm Otwell, 38.
Clyde Amos Stout, 57.
Aunt Tessie Johnson, 78.
Leon Powell, 10.
Jean Dianne Truce, 8.
Sammy Truce, 5.
Tommy Clayton Truce, 3.
Onnie Mitchell, 48.
Maxine Silvers, 31.
Tricia Bowen, 28.
Conner Lee Stevenson, 61.

Many others were hurt. Some were taken to the hospital at Whitt City, and some were taken to the Primitive Baptist Church. Brother Bob George, pastor, and Flank Busby went among the injured and the sorrowing, praying and talking with them throughout the dark and rainy night. Many asked for Shack. But Shack was out in the rain, helping find the bodies. He worked all night and all the next day, and the next night he visited the bereaved and the injured. His own house was hardly touched by the wind.

Shack had become a giant. The people watched him in awe and wonder. When he entered a house, talk stopped, and everybody watched him. They listened as he talked to the widows and the lame. His voice was quiet and low, and he moved with a new assurance. The people pressed close to hear what he would say, to watch him.

Scuppernong had been brought low, and only Shack had seen it coming; only Shack knew what it meant.

"Woe unto Scuppernong," Shack had said.

#

Chapter 19

The sun was shining the day of the funeral. Eleven graves had been dug in the cemetery at the foot of Cat Mountain. A mass service was held at Primitive Baptist Church.

> **"What a friend we have in Jesus**
> **All our sins and griefs to bear . . .**
> **What a privilege to carry**
> **Everything to God in prayer."**

Brother George was the first speaker. Then there was another song:

> **"Rock of Ages, cleft for me . . .**
> **Let me hide myself in thee."**

Then Brother Horace Nelson from the Methodist Church at Whitt City spoke, and Abner Wilcutt from the Holiness Church. Shack was the last speaker.

"My people," he began, "we must not weep too long for these here loved ones because we will see them all agin. We'll meet them on that other shore, and it won't be no long time coming. We'll see them agin on the other side in just a few more days, so let us not weep too long here today." He spoke in a quiet, strong voice, and the people listened closely.

The church was full, and others stood on the porch and in the yard. A baby cried, and somebody coughed. Muffled sobs spiked the air, and a sorrowful cry escaped from the crowd. But they heard Shack.

"Now this is a terrible happening, I won't try to tell you it ain't. The judgment of the Lord is always a terrible thing. But this here today is little bitty besides what the Judgment Day is going to be like. Why, this here's just a seed out of the pod besides what that's going to be. This here's just a warning to us who are left that the great day of judgment is coming. And people . . ."

He lifted his eyebrows and looked about gravely. "My people, if I know my heart, it ain't going to be far off."

Outside the sun was shining warmly. A jaybird flew into a tree beside the church, screaming, "Thief! Thief! Thief!" A small boy looked at the blue and white feathers, then back at the black hearses lined in a row.

"It's been a heavy burden on my heart," Shack said. "I've been wanting to tell you, but it's hard to tell a body something when he won't listen. I tell you, People, it's been a heavy, heavy burden on my heart." He surveyed the crop of heads and stepped away from the podium.

"I believe the day has come when you're ready to listen," he said. "I believe ever one of you will be still today and listen. I just feel like, People, that the Lord God of Abraham has set the appointed day, and it's been a burden on my heart. And I ain't told nobody what I'm about to tell all of you now." He spread his hands toward the caskets.

"These good folks have gone on ahead. Norm, Onnie, Conner Lee—all of them. They just gone on ahead. And in a few days, we will follow. In a very few days. The end of Time is coming, People, and I'm going to tell you when it is." He paused, surveying the anxious eyes.

"I'm not quite ready. The Lord is not ready to say the day. But He will reveal it soon. Listen. Listen to what I'm going to tell. I'm going to have to go away from you for a season. I'm going to go upon the mountain yonder, and I'm going to fast and pray for forty days and forty nights, and on the forty-first day I will give you the ainser. I want you all to come up on the mountain on the forty-first day to a tabernacle that I'm going to build. And on that day, we'll sing praises, and we'll pray, and then I'll tell you the day and the hour. The Lord will reveal it to me, and then you will know when the end will come. I want ever man, woman and child to come on the mountain to hear the word about Judgment Day."

He glanced all around the room, and then, in a triumphant voice, said, "My helper, Flank Busby, will show you the way. He will lead you to me, and then all of us—all who are ready—will go to be with these dear loved ones over on the other shore.

Chapter 20

Shack tried to talk to Pearl and Margaret before he left for Cat Mountain, but he failed. Nobody could talk with Margaret anymore. The only person she talked with was Margaret, and on the morning that Shack left, she sat in a corner of the kitchen talking to herself. She had made a doll out of an immature ear of corn, pulling the shucks back on each side, like a robe, and pretending the young soft silks were beautiful long hair. She held the toy in her lap and whispered to it, giggled, shook her head, and whispered some more.

Shack stood in the kitchen with an old tin suitcase in one hand and looked at his daughter. He wore a coat with a wilted flower in the lapel. "Baby," he said. "Daddy wants you to be a good girl while he's gone."

"We've got to do something with this hair," Margaret said to the tiny ear of corn. She hugged it tightly.

"You hear me, Baby? I'm going to be gone awhile, but Papa'll be back."

"You want a new dress?" she cooed. "I'll make you a whole bunch of new dresses."

"Papa loves you, Margaret. You be good while I'm gone to be with the Lord. You help Mama take care of the house. If you get sick, Mama'll get the doctor-man for you. You stay close to home, now." He looked a long while at her, but she did not return it. She acted as though she didn't know he was in the house.

"You're beautiful. You're plumb beautiful. I'll make you a new dress . . ."

"Papa loves you, Baby. Papa . . ."

Shack went into Peeter's old bedroom. Pearl was still in bed although morning was half past. Her hair needed combing. She raised her head off the pillow to look at him.

"I'm going," Shack said.

Pearl settled her face back on the pillow.

"I'm going to Cat Mountain for forty days and nights."

"Hallelujah," she muttered.

"Ain't you going to cook no breakfast?"

"I don't want none right now."

"You sick?"

Pearl moved again so she could see him.

"I'm going up on the mountain," he said.

She stretched and turned toward the wall. She heard his steps as Shack walked quickly through the house, and she heard the screen door slam. She lay very still.

She heard his heavy steps on the porch and on the gravel of the road. She did not cry. She listened to the noise her husband's shoes made on the gravel, as she had once listened to the rims of wagon wheels passing in the noonday and mules' hooves crunching.

Pearl no longer thought about housework and seldom swept the floors, and it had been weeks since she had mopped the old boards. She didn't plan meals either. She cooked whatever she found to cook, whenever she was hungry, and if Margaret didn't fix for herself, Pearl prepared enough for both of them, but they never ate together or with Shack.

Green beans hardened in the garden, and she did not gather them except a few from day to day; she no longer canned. Tomatoes ripened and great black circles formed on their bottoms, finally opening as trap doors to let the juicy insides fall away.

Well, all that's over with now, I reckon. Just me and her. And all she does is set and talk to herself. I wonder what will happen. What he will do.

I was just a girl. If I had it to do over with, I'd know better. Maybe. I don't know. March wind and sunshine and little flowers coming out and white blossoms on the plum trees and pink peach blooms. Then. And how was she to know what he would become?

Then he was strong and wiry and a happiness bubbled in him, and something like the peach blossoms. Calves had grazed in a pasture and how was she to know that some day he would treat his son like one of them?

He's so proud of his steers. Pure, he calls 'em. I wonder what on Earth he thanks would become of things if steers was all there was. Or if everbody quit doing what he used to thank was so fine.

I was just a girl. It was the spring after the summer I was babatized in Rainbow River. I can't hardly remember nothing else before then. And now that's done happened and gone, and he says the world's coming to an end, and what's there to do even if it don't? Just me. That was a long time ago, I reckon, but it don't seem long since I was a girl.

That day. Sunday afternoon. He wanted awful bad. I didn't even know for certain what he was getting at. Laying there on the pasture grass. Something terrible now, but that day it was jim dandy fine, I reckon. He acted like it was. Smiling and whimpering and all excited, and now he's gone on the mountain. *To pray.*

Ain't looked at me in no telling how long. Looked at me that day! His straw hat fell on the clover and rolled with the wind. He's gone. That's all over.

Standing there, saying funny thangs, and the old preacher with snuff on his lip and no coat looking over his brown glasses, and a lamp burning, and my stomach tight like it was going to bust, saying, "Well, Murphy, she's yourn now, kiss her," and him so frisky in bed in the back room at Mama's and then two nights later gone and probably over at Selma Cunningham's and always over someplace. Until Hoyt got runned over. Then praying and telling me what's wrong and what ain't. And worrying that the kids was going to do something bad.

He's gone.

And I reckon maybe the world is going to end someday, but I don't know what he's got to do with it. Treating my boy that a-way. Well, he's gone. Gone on the mountain.

I never minded him wanting even when I didn't. But then he didn't want even when I did. *Do.* I don't reckon I'm s'posed to. But all that's over and there ain't hardly nothing I can remember that he wasn't part of, but he's gone now. Nearly-bout everybody else is gone, too. Somewheres.

Pearl lay for a long time, trying to sleep and knowing she wouldn't and hating to get up and knowing that some time she would have to and finally deciding to go to Sam Antone Rose's house to see her son.

She saw Margaret bent in the corner of the kitchen, whispering to the little green object in her hands, but Pearl didn't look long because she couldn't. There was still enough left inside Pearl that wouldn't let her look long at her whispering daughter.

She opened a cabinet door and broke off a piece of biscuit and ate it as she went out the back. It was already hot outside, the coolness gone with morning dew. The road had not entirely dried since the storm, and in places Pearl left the print of her tennis shoes. She met Mr. Rod Amos as she walked, and he waved, and she waved to him. He hadn't changed, she didn't guess. He was one man who hadn't changed, from what they all said.

Pearl watched a blue-tailed lizard run in the grass beside the road, stop, and run again.

Peeter was sitting in a rocking chair on the front porch. He kept rocking as Pearl approached. "Where you going?" he asked.

"Nowheres."

"You want a drank?"

"Nah, that's all right." She perched on the edge of the porch with one foot touching the ground. "Well," she said, "your papa's gone up yonder."

"Up where?"

"Up on Cat Mountain. Said that's where he was headed."

"Maybe he'll get snake-bit."

"Law me," Pearl said, with a long sigh.

"What's he going to eat?"

"I don't know."

"Lizards, I reckon," said Peeter. "And toad frogs."

"He's going to stay a long time."

"I don't care if he rots up there."

"I reckon you don't."

Sam's bald-bottomed rooster chased a hen around to the front and rode her down. Pearl watched as the rooster got off and walked away, stiff-legged, and the hen rose to her feet, fluttered her feathers, and stood still.

"He's gone," Pearl said quietly.

"I hope a rattlesnake bites him."

"You look sickly."

"I ain't sick."

"You got no color."

"I don't need none."

"You need a purgative."

"Shoot-fire, just hush about it."

Sam came around from the back. "Well, look a-here. How you?"

"All right."

"What do you know, Pretty Lady?"

"Not much."

"Sam's building a gol-derned airplane, Mama."

"Ain't no airplane, now," Sam said. "It's a glider."

"That's what I meant. Down there in the barn. Wanta see it?"

"I don't care."

"I'll show it to you," Peeter said.

Pearl didn't answer.

"Let's go down there," Sam said. "I'll show you myself."

"Yeah, come on, Mama."

She cupped her chin in her hand, as she looked at the ground.

"I reckon she don't want much to," Sam said.

"Got too much on me to be looking in no barn," Pearl said.

Sam sat beside her. "Old Shack leave you?" he asked.

"Gone up on the mountain."

"What I heard," Sam said. "He's crazy. You too good a woman to just walk off and leave. You hear? What you gonna eat on?"

Pearl shook her head.

"My Lord, Woman, come down here with me and old Peeter. We'll feed you, won't we, Boy?"

Pearl grinned. "I can't come no place."

Sam laughed. "Why, just pack up your belongings and brang 'em on down. We'll put you up. Let old Shack worry about the end of the world if he wants to. You come live with me and the boy, hear?"

"I can't move nowhere," Pearl said. "I got to stay and look after Margaret."

"Brang her, too!"

Pearl snickered quietly, then giggled aloud.

"I mean it!" Sam said.

There was something bubbling in Sam, something in the way he talked that made her remember the white plum blossoms and pink peach blooms. And Shack. She looked away, to the pasture. Sam's bull—red, wavy hair and white forehead—was ambling toward the barn. Pearl noted his testicles, swaying heavily with each step.

"Come on," Sam said. "Sam'll show you."

They started across the pasture, past the rubber-tired wagon.

"Me and old Peeter get along good," Sam said. "He's a good boy, I can tell you."

"He oughta come home, I 'spect."

"What you talking about? I treat him like he was my own."

"I ain't going home!" Peeter said.

"You hear that! Get on away from here. Shoo! Git!" Sam waved the bull away so they could get into the barn.

It was dark inside, but Sam opened the big door at the end to let in light. The glider squatted low on the dirt floor beneath the hayloft. Sam rubbed his hand on the smooth wing. He was very proud of the wing that he had built with plywood.

"It ain't heavy," Peeter said.

"Where do you set at?" asked Pearl.

"I forgot to put a place to set," Sam said. "I got busy working on the wing, and I plumb forgot to put a seat in it. It don't make no difference. I probably won't never fly it nohow."

"How come you to build it, then?"

"Dadgumed if I know."

Sam stood very close to Pearl, thinking: She's pretty a woman as I ever seen. Not like the widow, either. I bet she's got some sense. *Wisht I had her in the hayloft.*

"It sure's hot," said Pearl.

"Why don't you go get your mama a drank?" Sam said.

"She don't want none."

"I bet she wants some now. Don't you want a drank?"

"That's all right," Pearl said.

"Run on and get her some water," Sam said. "Go on. Brang me some, too."

"Aw, y'all don't want no water."

"Go get us some, Peeter. Hear? I'm about to die of thirst."

Peeter walked off. He cupped his hands to his mouth and blew into them, making a sound like a dove. He turned at the door and looked at Sam. There was something in his voice that Peeter didn't like. He made the dove's call again as he walked away.

Sam kicked at hay near the glider. "Pretty, ain't it?"

Pearl nodded.

"You're pretty, too," Sam said.

Pearl looked away. His voice sounded like Shack's had sounded long ago. She smelled Sam close and thought he touched her.

"Awful pretty," Sam said.

"Ain't nobody said that in I don't know when," Pearl said. She thought: *He's funny looking. Wonder why he ain't got no eyelashes. But he talks good. Not mad-like.*

"I wouldn't run off and leave you, myself," Sam whispered. He was close behind her. She heard his breathing. Pearl felt him brush her hip. She moved slightly away.

Sam touched her elbow, steering her deeper into the barn. "You're a good woman," he said. "I always known how good you was. Shack ain't got a lick of sense."

"He's the one I marrit," Pearl said.

"I don't care. He run off and left you, didn't he?"

Pearl cupped her chin in her hand, covering her mouth with her fingers, and stared at the glider. *I ain't got no business down here,* she thought. *Only.*

"Sweet lady," Sam Antone Rose whispered from behind her. She felt something damp on her neck. Then his hands came around to clasp what no man but Shack had ever touched.

Pearl knocked his hands down.

"Come live here," Sam begged. "Move over here."

"Pshaw."

"I mean it!" Sam said.

"I done told you I can't move nowheres."

"Then I'm gonna come see you."

"Margaret . . ."

"Hellfar, I'll come after she goes to sleep!"

Pearl turned to face him—his amber eyes squinting through lash-less lids, leather cap tight on his cantaloupe-shaped head, begging like a tom-cat—that she should be there with this funny little man with that same urgency in his voice that she remembered from so long ago. And her crazy husband off on Cat Mountain somewhere, waiting for the world to end. She started laughing hysterically.

"What you laughing at?" asked Sam. "You see if I don't come over there. I don't care how late."

Pearl wouldn't stop laughing, so Sam joined in, too. Both were choking with laughter when Peeter came in with two peanut butter glasses of water. He stood staring till finally the laughter stopped.

"What's wrong with y'all?" Peeter asked. When they didn't answer, he said, "I spilled some."

"That don't make no difference," Sam said.

No one spoke while Sam and Pearl, staring at the glider, drank their water.

"Let's go back up yonder," said Peeter. "Hear?"

Pearl started out.

"Come on Sam," Peeter said. "Let's go back up yonder."

"All right, Bohunk," Sam said. "I'm right behind you."

"I'd like to know what's so gol-derned funny," Peeter said.

#

Chapter 21

Pearl wasn't sure she had been asleep when the dog started barking. Moonlight was on her bed. Maybe she'd dreamed it, but she thought someone had called her name. The name, the sound, was inside her head—had popped up there, but now everything was quiet save for the barking. She sat up. It might be *him*, she thought, come down from the mountain. For a second, this possibility excited her. Then she remembered.

She tip-toed barefoot to the back door, unlatched it, and peered into the shadowed yard. "Hush up!" she said, and the white dog wagged its tail and took a step or two out of the shadows. It looked like a ghost in the moonlight. "Hush your barking!" Pearl said and was closing the door when she saw the little man ease out of the darkness, his hand raised.

"Wait!" he whispered. "Pearl?"

O my Lord. She stepped barefoot into the yard.

"C'mere."

Pearl moved toward the oak's jagged shadows. "What on earth?"

Somewhere in the white yard Sam held her, stroking her hair, petting her as though she were a frightened child. She *was* trembling, partly from the after-midnight cool. He tried to kiss her, but Pearl kept her face tight against his chest—stuck there as though held by a magnet. Unmoveable. He kissed her face, her hair. "What?"

"I can't."

"Wha'chu mean?"

"I'm marrit."

"I know you are—to a fool who'd ruther sleep on hard ground than with his pretty woman."

"Don't make no difference," Pearl said. She struggled to get free of his embrace as Sam was trying to kiss her. "I got to see about Margaret."

"Honey, I want . . ."

"I know it, but turn me loose anyhow. I'm a marrit woman." She pulled free and turned her back to Sam, but she did not go away.

Sam swore quietly. "You don't care how much nobody wants, do you?"

"I'm Murphy's wife."

"Shack, you mean."

"I call him Murphy."

Sam was trying hard to be patient. "And you're scared a him."

"Un-uh," she said. "It ain't him." She mumbled something else.

"What'd you say? Huh? Tell me, Pretty Woman."

"I said I got babatized one time."

"Babatized?"

"In the river. When I was thirteen year old."

The white dog was sniffing at Sam Antone Rose's shoes. All the yard seemed bathed in light except for the crooked shadows. A cool breeze nuzzled Pearl beneath her flimsy gown.

"Git away, dog!" Sam said, stomping his foot. He rubbed his hand across his face. "I reckon I walked up here for nothing."

"I dint tell you to."

"You didn't run me off."

"I know it. That what you wanted?"

"Naw. But . . ." He whirled and took a couple of steps toward the road. He turned back, his voice, strained, going high, like a boy's. "I can't believe you'd . . . after the way he done that boy . . ."

Pearl moved close. She reached and touched Sam's arm. "Peeter told it, didn't he?" she whispered.

"Course he told me! Shack ain't fit for you, Pretty Woman."

"It was the most awfullest thang . . ." Pearl was crying. Sam pulled her to him and held her there for a long while. Petting. Comforting.

"You thank I don't know about wanting?" she asked.

"Tell me, Pretty Woman."

"You don't know the half of it," she said.

"You not wanting that old fart?"

"Hush up about him."

"Ain't you cold?" asked Sam.

She moved slightly, but did not answer.

"Say? This little old gown. You cold?"

She moved so she could see his face. "Sam?" Softly.

"Tell me, Sweet Bird."

She moved slightly, but found his hand.

"What? What is it?"

"Could we be quiet, you reckon?"

"What'd you say?"

"Could we be quiet?"

"Lord yes!" Sam said.

"We got to be," she whispered.

Sam visited Pearl the next three nights. On the last night, it was very late before he returned to his own bed. He couldn't go to sleep for thinking about her. Fierce little Pearl. She was like a stranger from the shuffling, plump little woman who had seemed so shy before. No woman had ever kissed Sam so hard as she did; none had been so rapacious. She was like an angry bob-cat, Sam thought. His fingers explored a burning spot on his shoulder, another on his neck. There were various other sore places. O my little cat, I love you. But it was not so easy to keep her quiet.

Sam wished that Shack would fall off the mountain and break his neck or at least never come back. I oughta sneak up there and knock him in the head. Then her and me and Peeter could slip off . . . well, there's Margaret. Setting around whispering all the time. Maybe we could send her off somewheres—she's just like him, not a lick of sense. Then we could go off. Maybe Peeter would call me Papa. And Pearl wouldn't never mess around on me. She's not really mad, neither. She loves me, too, she just won't say it. I know anyhow. I love her and told her so. She just holds on. And bites. She does act mad, if I didn't know better . . .

"Where'd you go last night?"

Look out now! I thought you was sleep.

"Say, Sam. Where'd you go?"

"Nowheres."

"Liar. I seen you."

"What you talking about?"

"I seen you go off down the road."

"Boy, I didn't go nowheres. You having bad dreams."

"I seen you."

"I just walked down the road apiece. Had the heartburn so bad, I couldn't sleep, so I got up and walked up and down the road. I didn't know you was awake, Bohunk."

"Lying sonbitch, I know where you went. Knowed that day in the barn . . . talking about being thirsty. Knowed what you wanted. And her making out like she's coming to see *me*. She ought not never have let *him* do what he done to me."

"Nah, I had heartburn," Sam said. "I just went down there a piece and turned around."

"Yeah, you. Calling me buddy and stuff. I gotta watch you, too."

Sam couldn't sleep even after Peeter got quiet. He counted buzzards circling, and grasshoppers jumping everywhere; still, he was wide awake. He was worried about everything—about Shack coming back, about what Peeter said, about whether Pearl had ever done like that with anybody else. And if she was really angry or what.

Suddenly, Peeter asked, "You know something?"

"Nah, I don't know a blessed thing, Bohunk."

"He's scared to death of grasshoppers."

"Who is?"

"Papa."

"How come?"

"I don't know how come. He just is."

"Grasshoppers won't hurt nobody."

"I know it. But he's scared to death of them. He's always been afraid of grasshoppers."

"He's crazy," Sam said. "Grasshoppers won't hurt nobody. He ain't scared of them."

"Says he is. Says they give him goose pimples. Says that's why he don't like you, 'cause you always got a bunch of grasshoppers."

"Shack don't know what he's talking about. He ain't got a lick of sense."

"One time he said the whole world was going to be eat up by grasshoppers."

"No!" Sam said. "Hoppers is good!"

"I bet we could scare the pure dee old crap out of him."

"Huh?"

"I bet we could run him off of that mountain."

Suddenly Sam was interested.

"You ever see a giant grasshopper, Sam?"

"No, and you ain't neither."

"If we had a great big old grasshopper and taken him up on the mountain and turned him loose, I bet it'd scare him to death."

"There ain't no giant grasshoppers in the world," Sam said. "I know as much about hoppers as anybody, and there ain't none big enough to do that."

Peeter lay quietly, and Sam thought he had finally gone to sleep. Then Peeter jumped out of bed and lighted a lamp.

"What in blazes gnawing on you?" Sam said. "I can't sleep with no light glaring."

"We got one!" Peeter said. "Out in the barn. We got us a big old giant grasshopper."

"You crazy as Shack," Sam said. "I'll swear the whole family's crazy as bumblebees."

"You can make him a head," Peeter said. "Make him a great big head and paint him green, and we'll take it up there and run him off the bluff."

"You talking about my glider? That what you mean? Why didn't you say so? Yeah, I could make him look like a grasshopper, I guess. Only that wouldn't scare Shack."

"It would was we to take it up on the mountain, and me fly it right down on top of him."

"You can't fly it," Sam said. "It ain't got no seat."

"I'll ride it. They going up there pretty soon, ain't they? Everybody 'posed to go up there, you said. The world's ending, and everybody's going up there to watch? Ain't that right?"

"Yeah, that's what he told them."

"And they'll do it, too. And while they all standing around listening about the world coming to an end, I'll fly that old grasshopper right over the top of them, and the old fool will break his neck trying to get away."

"It won't work," Sam said.

128

"How come?"

"How you going get a mule up there to pull it to get it in the air without Shack seeing it and knowing what you're doing? Besides, it may not fly, and there ain't no place for you to set."

"I don't need no mule," said Peeter. "It ain't heavy. I lifted it the other day. It's real light. You just make that grasshopper head, and I'll fix some straps on his belly and run along like a grasshopper and jump off up there and float right down on top of him right in front of everybody. Will you do it?"

"Why yeah," Sam said. "Yeah, I'll make him a frigging head, but I ain't going to jump off no mountain."

"I'll do the jumping," Peeter said.

#

Chapter 22

The fire had burned low on the mountain top. A small purple-tinted waver of flame breathed around the last chunk of wood, fluttering along the underside of it, over the little white ash-squares and past the charred places. Wind blew tiny sparks off the chunk and into the darkness.

Shack sat on the ground in front of the embers. There was no moon, and the stars were so far away they could be forgotten. Now and then wind blew and lifted old leaves briefly off the ground and pushed them against dry grass and then let them down again and went away. Scuppernong was far away. The whole world was far away.

The ground on Cat Mountain was hard and cold, and Shack had said it would soon be gone, swept away into the black night.

Near Shack's foot lay a stone, rough and dark with shadows darting across it. Shack wondered how long it had been there and where it came from, and if it was going away in a few days with the world and all its people, as he had said. The chunk of wood was going away; he could see the slippery soft purple tongue of fire taking it away like millions of other pieces of wood that had been and then had gone away, eaten by some other purple flame, or had rotted and dropped into the earth. *Scuppernong—the world—was going away, too.* But when?

In two days they would come for his answer. When? September twenty-eighth had stuck in his mind. It had been in his mind all along, and in the beginning he had been sure and certain, but now he wasn't positive. The ground was hard, the stones were old, the wind strange and powerful, and the dark sky was far away and silent, and Shack was alone. The world, the people, the thousand people and more whom he had always known—when? How?

Shack lay on his bed of leaves, wrapped a blanket about him and looked at the dark pool of ink out there. Wind passed over his face and down the side of Cat Mountain like a whisper: *When? When?*

Scuppernong. Scuppernong. Different in the heart of night. Shack thought of trout in Rainbow River and of a young farmer going from the fields to fish in the cool shade and of purple-black muscadines dropping into the water below the high bank where the fisherman had sat. He remembered young boys splashing in the shallows of the river and plunging into Fifteen-Foot-Hole and playing "hot-tail" on the bank, scampering, running with hands over white vulnerable butts and escaping in the cool river depths.

He thought of green fields of corn and warm dry wind-breezes and of water jugs under young sprouts and of horseflies on sweating mule-rumps and silver plows slicing black earth. He thought of pulling hard dusty green blades from cornstalks, filling both hands with the fodder and then tying the bundles with a long limber blade of corn and bending a stalk to hang the bundle to dry. He thought of gathering the dry brown bundles later and laying them on the ground across a stretched-out rope and carrying the greater rope-tied bundle to the barn and stacking the small hands of fodder row on row in a shadowy barn, and of the stinging on his neck and back from the fodder fuzz.

He thought of a rainy day in an old schoolhouse and of songs in a church. He thought of splitting kindling wood and sawing big green logs and smelling the rich oak and of stacking wood under a house.

He thought of chickens on a roost just before dark, of squealing hogs, thrusting their front feet in the cloudy slop water of a V-shaped trough, crowding, pushing, fighting for the white lumps and red tomato pieces and strings of potato peelings that floated in the cloudy water—of the damp fat teats of a cow and the tinging sound of milk hitting pail, and the foaming, rising fullness against the silver sides. *When?*

He thought of an electric fan humming on a store shelf in July, of a smoking fire on a cold day and a steaming black pot of boiling water in a back yard. He thought of putting a rifle bullet through the pone in front of a hog's head and slitting the sagging hairy throat with a knife and spilling the red thick blood and scraping the wiry bristles after scalding water and taking the entrails out rope by rope, and of fresh pork frying in a skillet, and warm gravy on split-open biscuits. *O Scuppernong!*

He thought of a boy in a cold room under a patch quilt and of a voice across the hall saying, "Git up, Murph! Git up, Boy, and build a farr!" And of walking in the cold thin morning to the fireplace and laying the thin yellow-brown streaked pine kindling in and lighting a match and then doing the same thing in the big stove in the kitchen. And again of the boy going into a big room on a cold Christmas morning when a fire was already roaring in the fireplace and taking a long sock from the mantel and hurrying to get the strange objects out of it—yellow oranges, red apples, striped candy. *Where? Who?*

Wind slipped across his face and down the mountainside.

Bit by bit, piece by piece, the drama that had been Scuppernong, the chronicle of Shack and all the people and things that had been a part of Shack through the long and brief years blew back to him, blew across him, and left him hollow and sad and lonely as the night, and it was all down below him in the heart of night, and it was all to blow away, all to end with no more sunshine, no more light, no more growing corn, no more flowing river, but all to blow away into the black and inky night, but when? *Why?*

Pearl. Kind and gentle and waiting, warm Pearl. Shack remembered a night, the night, when he had stood on their front porch, walked there, leaned against a post, sat in the swing, sat on the boards with his feet on the ground and heard her groans and heard her cries and finally, inside, cradled beside her in the warm stuffy dingy lighted room the wet, red wrinkled crying face of his Margaret. And Pearl, kind and gentle, shy and embarrassed, touching the wet little curls.

This, and of walking on damp quiet leaves early in the morning with a little boy, looking for squirrels. And of his mother dying in a back room with a lamp flickering and glowing, and of snow deep against the barn.

Shack got up and walked so he could see down there, but the few straggling lights told nothing. He looked again at the dying fire, and he stiffened because someone was coming toward him, coming from nowhere straight toward him. On the other side of the fire, he saw the movement.

Shack waited in the shadows, straining to see who it was, afraid, listening to the bold steps.

"Where'd you go?"

The flat loud woman's voice spoken matter of factly in darkness. "Hey, where'd you run off to?"

And Shack, who moments before had been wrestling with mysteries of his spirit, now recognized the approaching battle with the flesh, for the voice belonged to Mrs. Edna Marie Ophelia Brown. Shack recognized her even though they had never spoken to each other. "What is it, Sister?"

"Oh, I didn't know where you was! I knowed you was here somewheres because I seen you setting by the fire from back down yonder-way." She stopped beside the fire.

She wore a white blouse, a light sweater and blue slacks and a scarf was tied around her head. She bent and put some sticks on the red coals. Shack saw them snap into nervous fingers of flame.

"It's creepy up here, ain't it?"

Shack didn't answer.

"My bat-trees burned out down there 'fore I got to the top. I was scared I'd step on a snake."

"Why'd you come, Sister?"

"Oh, I had to. I wasn't doing nothing. Whew, it took my breath coming up that hill." She squatted by the fire and fed it more sticks.

Shack saw the shadows on her face. "Wasn't you scared, young woman?"

"It was pretty spooky! I was afraid I'd got lost."

"How'd you know the way?"

"I been here before. Ain't never been by myself, though, Buddy. I'll tell you, I won't never come back by myself neither."

"How come you here?"

"I just come. I wasn't doing nothing special."

She looked around and, seeing the leaf-bed, moved to it and sat. She hugged herself and shivered. "It's downright cold, you know it?" She pulled the blanket about her shoulders and looked at the fire.

Shack stepped closer. He placed a chunk of wood carefully on the fire. "Are you in trouble?"

"Naw. I don't get in no trouble. People all time mouthing about me, but I don't get in no mischief. Lots of them get in more mischief than I do. I got five kids, and I can't go getting in no trouble." She wore tennis shoes and white anklets.

"You get lonesome since you been up here?"

Shack looked at the full, thick-skinned face and the pug nose. Her lower lip was large, like a thick slice of ripe tomato. Her eyes were dark hollows.

"Yes," he said. He sat on the ground on the other side of the fire and clasped his hands in front of him. He turned the nub of his finger, studying it.

"They didn't do you right, letting you come off up here by yourself," she said.

"They didn't do it."

"They let you."

"I'm a preacher."

"Don't I know it!" She straightened her shoulders and leaned toward him. "I heard you," she said. "You know that day you was down at the courthouse that time? You remember the day you was playing with that ball of fire? I seen you that day."

"Did?"

"Yeah. That was good. I heard every word you said."

"Did you believe it?"

"Oh Lord yes. I don't never forget nothing, you know that? I always been like that. My brother used to say I made it up because he couldn't remember like I do, but I never made nothing up. I just remember. I remember ever word right now that you said down there that day. It was real good. It really was."

She untied the scarf while she talked and shook her head, scattering the loose brown waves of hair. Shack saw a strand flip across her wide forehead and swing slightly as she talked.

"They didn't do you right."

"It was my doings."

"That don't matter. No business letting a man come off up here all by his lonesome. That's why I come." She looked at Shack. "You know about me, don't you? Huh? You've heard what they say about me, I reckon."

She leaned forward and rested her mouth on her arm and bit it, lightly. "I don't care," she said. "I don't never get in no trouble. I don't care what they say, I wouldn't let nobody go off on a mountain and stay by their selves. I know that."

Shack took a deep breath.

"Anybody's good as you, they ought not do 'em that way. It don't matter what they say about me, but somebody that's good . . . you could get sick up here by yourself and nobody on earth would know it. You could! That's why I come."

Shack looked away. He stood and turned his back to the fire and looked out into the darkness. "What are they saying down there?" he asked.

"Huh? Oh, they talking about it."

"Have they forgot?"

"Forgot? Why Lord no. They know you're up here all right. That was good what you told them."

Mrs. Brown stretched out on the leaves and spread the blanket over her. "It's chilly up here," she said. "I bet you're cold."

Shack turned away. He looked over his shoulder at her. "You ought not be here," he said.

She flounced on the leaves, rooting her body into a more comfortable position.

"You better go on back now."

It was very quiet between them.

Mrs. Brown looked at the stars. She counted one hundred and seventy-five. Then she moved on the leaves and looked at Shack. He had turned to face her. She raised the blanket on one side. "Get under here," she said. "I know you're bound to be cold."

Shack frowned and started to speak, but instead he looked at the darkening coals.

"I thought about you up here by yourself," she said. "I said to myself, I'll bet that man is one lonesome human being. I said I'll bet he gets cold up there nights, and I was right. Brrr. It's chilly."

"You better go see about your kids."

"I said anybody that'd let a good man go off like that by his self, huh!"

Shack was looking at her, as though in a trance.

"I'm supposed to tell them," he said.

"I know it," she said softly. "They're worried sick about it." She laughed. "Buddy, you sure got 'em scared. Come on over here. There's enough blanket for both of us. Come on." She moved to one side.

"No ma'am, that's all right."

"You better get under here or you'll catch cold."

"It's just a little while longer."

"You'll take cold, though. You don't want to have no cold when they come. Get under here!"

"You say they're scared?"

"Lordy yes. You've got the britches scared off of 'em."

"Are you?"

"Here, just lay down on a little bit of it. I know you're tired."

"Are you scared?"

Mrs. Brown laughed. "Why, I reckon I am," she said. "Why sure." She chuckled. "You sure know how to scare a body. Come on now, you're shaking. I see you shaking."

"You better go on home," Shack whispered. He sat down near her. She turned the blanket down and unbuttoned her blouse. Shack didn't say anything.

"I'm getting cold," she said.

"Cover yourself up!"

Shack held his head between his hands.

"I didn't like them letting you come off up here by your lonesome," she said.

Shack's face was buried on his arms, which were propped on his knees. "They don't care," he said.

"It burned me up."

"That's good of you, Sister."

"Come on," she whispered.

The fire was nearly gone. They could still see coals, but they couldn't see each other. Shack heard her moving heavily on the leaves, heard the shucking, peeling sound of her slacks until she was quiet again; quiet except for her whispers.

Shack felt wind in his face.

It was very dark, and he couldn't see the trees or the rocks, only stars and the black soup surrounding them. He couldn't see *her*. He couldn't see Scuppernong or the world. There was only the persistent whispers of Edna Marie Ophelia Brown saying, "Come on now. Come on. It's warm under here."

There were only a few tiny sparks on the underside of cooling wood-pieces when he felt his way, crawling, to the leaves and to the blanket.

#

Chapter 23

After the storm had passed, and Pearl lay drowsy and docile beside him in the darkness, Sam said, "You going up there?"

"Up where?" Pearl asked sleepily.

"Up on Cat Mountain. It's day after tomar."

"Don't reckon I've lost nothing on Cat Mountain," Pearl said.

"'Lowed you might want to know when the world's gonna end. *He's* gonna tell everybody, you know."

"I heered about it."

"I 'lowed you might be getting lonesome to see him anyhow," Sam said, trying to tease. He poked her in the ribs till she slapped his hand away.

"You ain't sleepy, why 'on't you go on home and let me sleep?"

"I may not get to come tomar night," Sam said. "You hear?"

"Well."

"Me and Peeter got some work to do."

Sam and Peeter had worked hard on the glider. They had applied the last coat of paint the day before. Sam was about to pop to tell Pearl their plans, but he had promised Peeter he wouldn't. As the time drew closer, Sam was as excited as Peeter about their scheme to scare Shack. He sure hoped his little glider would fly. He hoped Shack would break his neck or else get so scared he'd wind up three counties away.

"You hear me?" Sam asked.

"You ought not come no more, Sam."

"What you talking about! You just chewed my ear half-off and now you saying I ought not come back?"

"It don't feel right," Pearl said.

"What? What ain't I doing, Sweet Bird?"

"You do good," she said. "But it don't feel right."

"You act mightily like it does . . ."

"After, I mean."

"You mad at me or what? Huh?"

"No Honey, I couldn't get mad at you. But you ought not come back no more. It ain't right."

"Who says, Shack? You been listening to that wild man again?"

"No. I ain't listened to him in I don't know when. Why'nt you go on home now. Hear?"

"Well, shit-fire then, I'll go. If that's what you want. I bet you change your mind soon's it's dark agin."

As he was leaving, Sam heard Margaret, somewhere in the dark house, talking to herself. It was downright spooky.

Some time later, as it was starting to get light inside the house, Margaret went to Pearl's bed. She stuck her latest corn-shuck doll close to Pearl's face. "Wake up, Ma'am," Margaret said, using a falsetto voice.

Pearl, who was not sleeping, faced her daughter. "Whatcha want, Baby?"

"Was that Papa?" Margaret asked.

"Why no," Pearl said. "Papa's not here."

"Oh. I thought I heard him talking."

Pearl reached out and felt of Margaret's tangled hair. "Papa's gone, Dumpling," she said. "Member? He's gone up on the mountain."

Margaret responded with a little laugh. She said something to her doll. Then to Pearl she said: "Victoria wants to be babatized."

"Who does . . . oh."

"Down in the river like you was," Margaret said.

Pearl looked long and hard at her daughter. "You member that? I told you that a long time ago." She slid over and patted the bed beside her. "You want to lay down with me?"

"You said they ducked you way under."

"Lay down with me," Pearl said.

Margaret hesitated. "He won't get mad, will he?"

"Wye no, Dumplin. Don't you worry about him."

Slowly, Margaret stretched out, lying very close to the edge of the bed—careful not to touch her mother. She stroked the silks of her make-believe doll. "Was you big?"

Pearl lay on her side, facing Margaret. "I was thirteen year old."
She hesitated, remembering. Quietly: "I had let Jesus come into
my heart, so Brother Isaacs babatized me in Rainbow River."

"Was you scairt?"

"No!" Pearl said. "It was the most beautifulest day in my life.
The birds was sanging. And the water was bubbling there where it
dropped into this deep hole. And I smelt Sweet Shrub in the air."
She paused, glancing slyly at her daughter. "I felt clean as a scalded
fruit jar. And I thought ever thang was gonna be awright for the
rest of my life."

"Oh Mama," Margaret said, calling her "Mama" for the first
time in a long time. "I wish I had been down there with you that
day." She reached and her fingers played in Pearl's hair and then
strolled on her cheek. At first, Margaret didn't know why the tips
of her fingers felt wet.

#

Chapter 24

Sam and Peeter went into the barn lot near midnight to harness one of Sam's mules. The moon was shining, and long shadows stretched away from the barn. It was damp and chilly. Peeter hitched the mule to Sam's rubber-tired wagon and led the animal to the front of the barn. Sam opened the big door. It dragged noisily across the ground. Sam held a lantern.

He and Peeter went inside, and Sam lifted the lantern high as they looked at the great grasshopper they had made. The body was painted dark green. Peeter touched the bright yellow wings. "Buddy, how about *that*!" he said.

Great eyes stared wildly from the large head that Sam had carved. The head had been painted green, too, and the eyes were white with large red pupils. Two small iron rods formed the antennae. Sam and Peeter stood quietly looking at the giant. Then Peeter scooted underneath, lifted, and with Sam guiding, walked outside, and loaded it onto the wagon.

"I hope she flies," Sam said.

"Don't worry, it will."

Two leather straps were slung underneath with hand-grips attached to the bottom of the wings. Peeter had practiced how he would fly the contraption, wiggling into position between the straps and the glider and gripping the leather pieces.

"May be too heavy," Sam said.

"Light as a feather," said Peeter. "I bet you a hunert dollars she'll fly."

The rubber tires of the wagon whispered on the gravel. Peeter took the reins from Sam and slapped them across the mule's back, forcing him into a trot. Peeter looked back at the glider. "Look at it!" he said. "Look! Ain't she a pretty thing?"

"What if nobody shows up?"

"Huh! Don't you worry, they'll be up there. Wouldn't miss it."

The mule was trotting along nicely under a quarter moon half-hidden by dark clouds. The old Pontiac wheels that Sam had adapted to the wagon were wobbling slightly, but the tires were not noisy on the graveled road. There'd be even less noise on the mountain trails, Peeter thought. He giggled.

"Wonder what the old jackass is doing now. Oughta be sleeping because he won't sleep none after this. Scared as he is over them little bitty grasshoppers, he won't never stop running from this baby."

They were quiet then. The grassy road was getting steep as they started up Cat Mountain. The lantern was on the seat between them, its flame flickering nervously. The trace-chains tightened, and the little mule dug his hooves into the dirt as he pulled against the slope. The moon had moved higher. Sam's heart wasn't in it anymore. All day he had worried about Pearl and their conversation of the night before. It felt like only a bad dream. Maybe she didn't mean any of it. He wouldn't know until he saw her again. So what was he doing on this wild goose chase!

"You sure you want to do this, Peeter?"

"Mighty right."

"Maybe he's changed."

Peeter didn't answer.

"Maybe you like Papa after all?"

"Giddap," said Peeter although the little mule hadn't stopped. Trees and bushes crouched darkly on each side of the rutted track.

"You know which way to go?"

"Yeah. Like I said, we'll wind around to the back side of the mountain and come out up above where the old fool's camped."

"You sure?"

"I told you, I been up here twict. I know 'zactly." Peeter clucked to the mule. "I hate his guts," he said.

"I ain't staying," Sam said.

"Why? You don't wanta see me fly it?"

"I got work to do. Besides, you don't want this old mule standing around up there making racket."

I know where you going, thought Peeter. He slapped the mule's rump hard with the reins.

After awhile the little road leveled and then forked, with the narrow route winding higher. They followed this one.

"He's down that other road," Peeter whispered. "Blow out that lantern."

They rode on in the dark as the twisting passage curved higher. Suddenly Peeter pulled back on the reins, and they stopped. "See?"

"Where?"

"Looky down there, through them bushes. See it?" Their shoulders touched. "Down there. See his far?"

"I see it," Sam said.

Small red coals glowed. "He's down there," whispered Peeter. "He's down there someplace. He's got a bunch of rocks stacked up close to the cliff. I seen it the other day."

Far beyond the campsite, Sam saw a light shining from some porch in Scuppernong.

"How you gonna get over these trees?"

"There ain't none on up yonder hardly."

Slowly they moved along the slim roadway. Grass grew high in the center, between the white ruts. The wagon jerked as the wheels dipped into a hole or struck a stump. Then they stopped.

"Right over yonder's where we need to set it," Peeter said. "On that bank. I can get a running start there. See? If you can hep me get it up that bank, I can get a running start and go right over them little bushes and smack into where they gonna be." His voice was trembling. "Wait'll he gets wound up, then I'll go sailing this old grasshopper right over the middle of them bushes. He'll break his gol-derned neck!"

"What if somebody sees it setting up here?"

"They won't. I'm gonna pile grass on it."

They unloaded the glider. Chains of the wagon creaked as the wagon rolled backward slightly. The mule snorted.

"He's going to hear us!" Sam said.

"Let him hear. Maybe he'll think it's a big old grasshopper farting." He was giggling, almost uncontrollably.

"Shhh," Sam warned. "He'll hear you, Bohunk."

"Maybe it'll give him a stroke!"

Finally they got the glider up on the bank.

"That's good," Peeter said. He crawled under and slipped into position and showed Sam how he could move it. "All I got to do is run," he said.

"You better run plenty fast," Sam said.

They sat on the ground, talking.

"You don't get hurt."

"I won't."

"You not gonna feel bad?"

"No," Peeter whispered. "I hate him."

"Don't do it if you gonna feel bad."

Peeter wished it wasn't true what he thought about Sam and his mother. In the moonlight, he could almost forget that. He wished the other wasn't true, either, but it was true forever. Thinking about it made him feel like hollow wood inside.

In a little while, Sam put his hand on Peeter's knee and gripped it. He leaned close and looked into Peeter's face. In the moonlight Sam looked like a stranger, except for the round cap. His eyes were huge.

"Be careful, Bohunk."

"Awright."

"You scared by yourself?"

"Nah." Peeter spat into the darkness. "I ain't scared."

"I'll see you when you get back then."

"You can stay you want to."

"I better get on back."

"Stay you want to. Hear?"

"I better not, Bohunk. Somebody might got a lonesome cow needs bulling."

"I bet."

"So long, Bohunk."

Peeter felt lonely and afraid as he watched the wagon disappear into shadows. It made more noise than he had expected, and then it was gone, and only the ringing quietness was left. Peeter cut some bushes and put them on top of the glider and then sat, thinking. He thought he knew where Sam had gone. And why.

After awhile the blackness drained from the sky, leaving it pale and anemic. Tiny blood vessels from the coming sun ruptured and bled pink against the clouds over Scuppernong. A brown thrush popped up on a limb beside Peeter and clucked. Suddenly the sun bobbed up from nowhere into the opaque soup, clear and free and shining bold.

Another day had dawned; the great, eternal machine that Shack had said would soon run down had performed its function perfectly another time. And Shack, Peeter noticed by moving to one side and peering over the top of a Sumac bush, was up and had performed a simple function, too. He saw Shack go to the rock pile and kneel.

Peeter was hungry. Some of the apprehension that he had felt in the chilly darkness had gone with the coming day, and he watched with eagerness the movements of his father. He looked forward to the flight. He lay on his back, waiting.

It grew into a warm day. It was like a holiday in Scuppernong. Stores closed. Nobody picked cotton. Nobody repaired fences. Steve Earley's cow bawled her signal that she and Nature were ready, but Steve let the day pass without taking her to a bull.

Sam Antone Rose stood in his house and watched the people pass on their way to the mountain. There was a steady stream until mid-morning. Many people walked. After awhile they stopped going by. Sam, shaved and scrubbed, put on a white shirt and tie, locked his house, and walked down the road away from Cat Mountain.

He was eager to see Pearl, to clear up all that crap from the last time. Maybe Margaret would have gone to the mountain, too, so they could be alone. But Margaret wouldn't bother nobody no way. Sam walked fast and chuckled at the thought of Peeter riding the big grasshopper over the heads of Shack and his followers.

"The world is ending, the world is ending," Sam sang softly. "The world is ending all day long."

As Pearl's house came into view, Sam didn't see the car immediately. At first he just saw the overall scene: the old house, the barn, the big oak trees and bare yard. Then the black car fell loose in the picture so that he couldn't see anything else. It was pulled off the road, sitting at the edge of the yard, coated with dust. *The mailman's car.*

A choking swelled in Sam's throat, but he quickly subdued it. A package, yes, that was all. Mr. Rod had just stopped to deliver a package. Then he saw that the mailman was holding the car door open and . . . Pearl, yes Pearl was crawling into the back seat! Yes, crazy Margaret, too.

Blindly, clumsily, Sam stumbled along the roadside, his eyes on the approaching car. Mr. Rod tooted his horn sharply as they passed Sam, but Pearl, sitting in the back seat on the side next to Sam, didn't even look. *Didn't even look!*

Sam's head was spinning, his vision as black as if his eyes were squeezed shut. In this darkness he stood screaming curses at the top of his lungs. Floundering, he fell, sprawling, in the roadside ditch and lay there awhile, crying. Two or three cars had passed, none stopping, but somebody tooted a horn—sickening, insulting, taunting toot exactly like Mr. Rod's—and one young voice had yelled: "Better lay off that rot-gut!" Finally, Sam got up and started trudging back down the road he had traveled.

Home again, the little man pulled clothes from the closet and stuffed them into a sack. He went to the bed where he had slept and lifted one of the round metal legs off the floor, stuck a finger up into the hollow leg, and fished out some paper money. He did the same at each of the bed's legs.

In the kitchen, he tore open a brown paper sack and spread it on the table. With a flat carpenter's pencil, he wrote in big letters on one side of the paper: "Goodbye Bohunk. This ur house now. Bull and mule and all thet is urs. And strawburies to. SAM R. And hoppers." Then he smashed his fist against the wall, drew back and smashed again.

Sam closed the door without locking it. He walked across the yard, his little leather cap pulled low on his head, and the paper sack of clothes cradled in his arm.

Softly, just above a whisper, he sang, "Nobody's darling on earth—nobody cares for me . . ."

#

Chapter 25

Peeter lay hidden under bushes while the people sang hymns. It was a big crowd. Peeter was hungry and thirsty, but they kept singing. Voices came to him, and Peeter liked the tune. It made him sad. He fished around in his pocket and found his little purple piece of bottle. But it didn't feel right today, and when he held it up and looked through it at the sun, it didn't look as good as it once had.

**"Gather with the Saints at the riv-ver
that flows by the throne of God."**

The words came clear and strong. Peeter wondered what the throne of God looked like. He thought of a huge white stone. The songs made him remember days when he was small and had gone to Vacation Bible School. He thought of the grape Kool-aid in tiny paper cups and remembered sitting in little chairs every day while Miss Jeanie told them stories about Jesus doing good things for people and helping a little girl get well. He had liked those stories. He wondered why Shack never told those things rather than what he did tell. He wondered, too, what had happened to Miss Jeanie, who kissed him on the forehead one morning. She didn't live around there but went to college somewhere.

Down there now, Shack was kneeling before a stack of rocks and many of the people were kneeling, too. They all looked to Peeter like children, playing a game. But they were not children. Suddenly it occurred to Peeter that they were all the *other* people. And they were small, gnarled, hard people who said and did dumb things and worked their tails to the bone, got sick, and died. They also snapped beans and canned tomatoes and milked cows and plowed and fished and hunted and sang hymns and cared for the sick and sat up with the dead. They were good enough, Peeter thought, though some drank rot-gut liquor and cussed and stole and lied, and most all of them did what Shack thought was so bad and what Peeter had never done and now would never do but what they had to do else there would be no one to swarm over the hillside to get the terrible message from his father.

The figures moved slowly in the sunshine, heads bobbling in talk, hands moving white handkerchiefs across sweaty faces. Here was Scuppernong, creation and creatures, all that Peeter had known, gathered in a clump on a still and rocky mountain.

In a way it was true what Shack had said: It *was* ending. Their little world was ending, and all of those people were going away. They would all soon be gone, and just the silent rocky mountain top would be there, washed with rain and swept with wind and holding in the sunshine like an empty boat on a river. And Papa, his wavy hair parted in the middle—Papa, with the chopped-off finger, would be dead. It was all true. Their world would end, and the plowing, the corn-chopping, cotton-picking, and the cursing, liquor-drinking, breeding (which Papa hated so) would all pass away. It was true after all.

Watching, Peeter felt suspended from them all, and he was sad. He reached back in his mind for somebody to love, but there was no one there. It was like coming home and finding your house burned down.

Sam's no friend of mine, sneaking out in the night, and I know where to, then letting on like he's my friend. I oughta cut his throat some night. Only I'm not going back to his house. I'll get even, though. I'll think about that after I finish doing this. And Mama. She had gone away like Margaret. They had gone so far away from Peeter that he didn't know how to find them anymore. Peeter felt oh so cold.

There's nobody left that's worth anything. All the people down there—I don't care about none of them. *He would not think about Lily.* I guess Papa don't care about nobody either is how come he tries to make his own people.

Down there now Flank Busby moved among the crowd, talking with the people, quoting Scripture, and praying. He looked very happy. From time to time he would go and hunker beside Shack and talk with him.

Eventually Shack called the people close. Scraggly whiskers covered his face. His hair curled above his collar. His face was thin, and his eyes looked like overripe muscadines. He had considered leaving before daylight. Now he could not leave. Now he had to try to find the old Shack. Try to go back to what he had before *she* took it from him three nights ago. To be strong and good again. Only he knew that he was neither. He knew also that he could not make them good. He knew now that he would never be able to make them good because he couldn't even be good himself. So maybe the world would end. Since none of them could be good, the world *had* to end.

"My people," Shack said, looking into the faces. "My faithful people." The muscadine were swimming now. "I have come away from you for forty days and forty nights. I have come here to be with the Lord. But the devil has been in my midst." He ducked his head and stared at the ground.

"Just as he tempted the Redeemer on that other mountain, he has tempted me. People, I've wrestled him. But you have been faithful. You have done what I said do, and come to hear about the day of judgment."

His voice became stronger, more confident, as he lifted his head and looked out over the crowd of people from Scuppernong.

"Judgment Day is coming!" he shouted. "Fire will rain from the skies and lick up this old sinful world, and thunder will roll and . . ."

Peeter pulled the bushes off the fake grasshopper. He slipped into the harness and pressed his back against the bottom board of the glider. He gripped the small leather straps and tested his strength. He felt the glider give with his flexing. He was scared, and his stomach was churning. He no longer knew why he was there.

It looked like a long way to where the people stood in a circle. Peeter moved his feet, getting a good feel, planting them firmly on the ground.

"All right now, Buddy," he mumbled. "Yeah now Buddy, we going to see now. All right now . . ." He pushed himself off and ran down the bank and jumped. His feet and legs—his entire body— dangled awkwardly, and the strap cut deep into his stomach, but he was no longer on the ground.

The people seemed so close.

I'm falling on them! I ain't flying, I'm falling! Look at them run!

Quickly, the glider careened above the crowd and smashed into a huge oak tree on the down side of the cliff and jerked Peeter roughly in the harness as it dragged him through the limbs. He wiggled loose and crawled around so he could sit on top of the glider. His face was bleeding.

Shack had been the first to see the big grasshopper and while he stood staring—before he broke and ran—several other people saw it, too. Men and women screamed as the crowd scrambled. Shack had run, looking back and crying: "The Judgment! The Judgment!" And he had plunged off the steep slope of the mountain and tumbled over rocks and rolled until stopping near the tree where the broken glider rested. His ankle felt like a shattered dish.

He heard voices above him. Several people came to the edge of the cliff and stared at him and at Peeter sitting in the tree. At first they were quiet. Then everyone seemed to be talking at once:

"Why, it ain't nothing. Just old Peeter."

"Look at him stuck up in that tree."

"Is Shack hurt?"

"Nah, he ain't hurt. Tried to fool us. Ain't no judgment. It's just his chap in that all-fired contraption."

"By Grannies, Shack sure run, didn't he? Huh?"

"Don't go down there. Shoot. Let 'em get out best way they can. Tried to trick us."

"Scared him worse'n anybody."

"World ain't coming to no end."

"Let's go home!"

"I got cotton to pick."

"I got a room full of arning."

"Let's git. Leave him down there."

"Yeah. He's got some praying to do."

"Scared of a dadgum old wooden grasshopper."

Flank Busby turned away from the cliff. He ran toward the crowd. "Wait!" he pleaded. "Wait. We'll have a meeting. We'll have a meeting tonight! I'll build us a brush arbor." He ran alongside the people as they scurried off the mountain. "Listen," he begged. "Listen. We'll have a meeting . . ."

But Flank's voice was lost in the din as the people made their way back to Scuppernong to resume living out their lives.

Chapter 26

One by one they went away until there was only Peeter, crouched on top of the splintered glider, and his father lying on the ground. Wind blew, and leaves flicked back and forth around Peeter's face, and he knew where his father was. He heard him moan and thought perhaps he was *dying*, and this was like thinking maybe the world was ending, for Shack was his father forever and ever.

The wind blew cool against Peeter's neck, and he felt the tree swaying, and far down the mountain tree tops squatted like grassy clumps and houses looked like play things, and only he and his father were left.

Well, I scared him, he thought. And run all his people off.

The wind was cold against Peeter's neck as it blew off the mountain toward the valley. The great wooden eyes of the fake grasshopper stared in the leaf cluster like some paralyzed monster.

"Lord, Lord," moaned Shack.

Peeter turned so that he could see his father sprawled on the rocky ground. One leg was twisted under Shack's body, and his arm shielded his face from the sun. He looked very small.

There was no fun in it now. The people were all gone. Shack's people had all gone home. But it was not funny now.

"Get down out of there," Shack said.

"Who said to?"

"Get your ass down from there."

"Why? So you can *kiss* it?"

"You better do like I say."

"I ain't never doing like you say again."

"Get down here and hep me."

"I ain't hepping you!"

"If my leg waddn't broke, you'd get down. I'd get you down!"

"What else could you do? Huh? Tell me, Old Man, what else do you think you could do to me? Kill me? Is that what you'd do?"

Fury overtook him, choking him, and Peeter started cursing, using words he'd never used before, making them up, screaming them in an incoherent torrent until he was drained of breath.

"I just wanted you to be good." Shack kept saying this.

Finally, Peeter's voice came back. "You wanted ever body to be good! You couldn't stand thinking about one of us doing nothing bad, could you? Naw, you old sonbitch, you couldn't let nobody do nothing 'sides what you wanted. Naw, naw! You just had to . . . to . . ."

"I just wanted you'uns to be good," Shack whimpered. "And to be good myself."

"Yeah. That's right! You don't care what you done to nobody long as you can say it was on account of being good. It wasn't good doing what you done to me. You hear me? *What you done to me was the worsest thing anybody ever done. Or* could ever do! You hear?"

"I was afraid what might happen," Shack said. "I had to do it on account of what might happen."

"What in the gol-derned hell worse coulda happened? Huh? Tell me, you crazy old fool."

"I didn't want nobody else to go to Hell," Shack said.

Peeter laughed, then, long and shrill and without mirth. It was a sad, frightening, awful laugh, as chilling as the wind.

"Honor thy father and thy mother," Shack intoned, "that thy days may be long upon the Earth . . ." Shack's voice was like the lonesome breeze, and Peeter no longer heard the words, only the sound and so did not hear when Shack said, "I oughta not done it, I don't reckon."

Peeter found the piece of purple glass in his pocket and without looking at it, sailed it far out over the tree tops, which he could not clearly see, for he was crying.

He sat very still in the cool sunshine, crying for all that might have been, and for all that could never be. Finally, he dropped down and went running as fast as he could down the side of the mountain.

#

Chapter 27

"I'm glad you flagged me down," Mr. Rod said, glancing over his shoulder at Pearl. He had wanted to move the mail bag from the front seat so Pearl could sit there, but she stopped him, saying she and Margaret would ride in back.

"Ought not of, I don't reckon," Pearl said. "And you trying to work."

"Foot!" Mr. Rod said, "Ain't nobody getting no mail today to speak of nohow. I'd lot sooner be riding with two pretty women. I kinda wanted to see what all the hullabaloo up there was about anyhow."

"Looks like it must be over," Pearl said.

"Yeah, they dribbling back down," the mail carrier said. They had met a few cars and now small groups were straggling down from the mountain. They seemed pretty happy, Pearl thought.

Margaret had braided her hair in two stiff pigtails that stuck out behind. She had kept asking about Shack until finally Pearl suggested they go find him. Now she stared through the window and said nothing.

"I bet old Shack gave 'em a good show!" Mr. Rod said.

As they rounded a curve, fairly high on the route, they saw a man run out in the road, waving his arms and yelling for them to stop.

"That's Flank Busby," Pearl announced.

"Sure is. What's he so worked up about?"

Mr. Rod stopped and Flank leaned close to his window. He was out of breath. "I'm glad to see y'all," Flank said. "I need y'all's help."

"What's wrong?" asked Mr. Rod.

"Brother Shack's hurt," Flank said.

"Well, get in."

"Wait," Pearl said, opening the back door. "You set back here, Flank."

He stared at Margaret. "Nome, I'll set up front."

"I said you set back here," Pearl said. "I'm getting up front. Move that mail bag. Can't you put it back in the trunk?"

"Sure can!" answered Mr. Rod, grabbing the bag and jumping out to open the trunk.

"Mama!" cried Margaret. "Mama, Papa said . . ."

"I don't care what he said. Go on, Flank. Git in here."

Reluctantly, Flank crawled in and sat beside Margaret. He was still breathing hard. Once they were moving again, Pearl said, "Now, tell me what happened."

"Brother Shack was preaching, he was, when all a suddent Peeter come flying over us, and it scared Brother Shack so bad he run off the mountain and hurt hissef."

"Whatchu mean 'flying'?" asked Pearl. "Peeter can't fly."

"He was certainly flying," Flank said. "He was hanging onto this great big grasshopper and . . ."

"Thunder," Pearl said. "The heat's got to him." She turned and faced him. "How bad hurt is Murphy? Just tell me that."

"I thank his leg's broke," Flank said. "He's laying off down there with one leg bent under him. I tried to hep him up, but he's too heavy."

"Is he by hissef?"

"Just him and Peeter," Flank said. "It was just them when I left to try to get some hep."

"What was Peeter doing?" Pearl asked.

"Just setting up there in a tree," Flank said. "I knowed I couldn't get Brother Shack outta there by myself, so . . ."

"Everbody else run off and left him?"

"Ever last one of 'em," Flank said. "And him laying there a-moaning for hep."

"I reckon we can hep you get him out of there," Pearl said. "I reckon all of us together can." She cupped her chin in her hand and glanced at Mr. Rod. "I'll be obliged if y'all will hep me git him home."

Mr. Rod chuckled. "You right sure you want to take him home, Pearl?" She turned away, toward the window. "Say, Pearl? You sure . . ."

"If he'll act halfway decent, yeah," Pearl said just above a whisper. She saw a cluster of small birds flying away from trees on the mountainside, climbing, dipping, sweeping here and there as one living body, lifting away from the trees, then returning. They seemed so very happy.

Pearl glanced at Margaret. Then she looked at Mr. Rod. "I can't just leave him to die up here on top of a mountain, can I?"

"I guess not, Pearl."

"I'm still marrit to him, you know."

"Let's see what we can do," said Mr. Rod.

As they moved on up the steep mountain road, Pearl heard Flank's hoarse whisper: "Gahhh, lookit them birds, Margaret!"

"I see 'em," Margaret said.

CPSIA information can be obtained at www.ICGtesting.com
Printed in the USA
LVOW06s1110160813

348059LV00001B/2/P